CONTROVERSY!

Religion and Government: Should They Mix?

Karen Judson

Marshall Cavendish
Benchmark
New York

Special thanks to Barry Hankins, professor of History and Director of Graduate Studies in the Department of History at Baylor University in Texas, and Nathan Oman, assistant professor in the Marshall-Wythe School of Law at the College of William and Mary in Virginia, for their expert review of this manuscript.

Marshall Cavendish Benchmark
99 White Plains Road
Tarrytown, NY 10591
www.marshallcavendish.us

Library of Congress Cataloging-in-Publication Data

Judson, Karen, 1941-
Religion and government : should they mix? / by Karen Judson.
p. cm. — (Controversy!)
Includes bibliographical references and index.
ISBN 978-0-7614-4235-6
1. Church and state—United States. I. Title.
BR516.J83 2009
322'.10973—dc22
2008044483

Publisher: Michelle Bisson
Art Director: Anahid Hamparian
Series Designer: Alicia Mikles

Photo research by Lindsay Aveilhe and Linda Sykes,
Linda Sykes Picture Research, Inc., Hilton Head, SC

Cover photo: Willfried Gredler/INSADCO Photography/Alamy

The photographs in this book are used by permission and through the courtesy of:
Mark Wilson/CNP/Corbis: 4; The Granger Collection: 12, 28, 60, 67;
Melanie Stetson Freeman/Christian Science Monitor/Getty Images: 50;
Getty Images: 53, 72, 104; ©Scher/SV-Bilderdienst/The Image Works: 69;
©Sanford/Aglioio/Corbis: 76; Christoher Morris/Time & Life Pictures/Getty Images: 80;
epa/Corbis: 88; Abedin Taherkenareh/epa/Corbis: 91; Charles Platiau/Reuters/Corbis: 95;
Bettmann/Corbis: 97; Regis Bossu/Sygma/Corbis: 106.

Printed in Malaysia
3 5 6 4 2

Contents

Introduction

FORMER PRESIDENT GEORGE W. BUSH, PERHAPS MORE often than some U.S. presidents who preceded him, frequently expressed his belief in God and invoked God's blessing. In keeping with his often-proclaimed religious faith, as president, Bush, for the first time in the nation's history, established a government office to oversee the distribution of government funds to "faith-based initiatives." The executive order establishing the White House Office of Faith-Based and Community Initiatives (OFBCI), stated in part:

> Faith-based and other community organizations are indispensable in meeting the needs of poor Americans and distressed neighborhoods. Government cannot be replaced by such organizations, but it can and should welcome them as partners. The paramount goal is compassionate results, and private and charitable community groups, including religious ones, should have the fullest opportunity permitted by law to compete on a level playing field, so long as they achieve valid public purposes, such as curbing crime, conquering addiction, strengthening families and neighborhoods, and overcoming poverty.

In 2008, then-president George W. Bush welcomed Pope Benedict XVI, the leader of the sovereign of the state (Vatican City) of which the Roman Catholic Church is the center, to the United States.

5

Bush's first presidential campaign stressed "compassionate conservatism"—a policy that recommended that community organizations, including religious groups, have access to federal money for the purpose of providing certain beneficial social services. The OFBCI provided opportunities for such groups to apply for federal grants, which could then be used to help people in need.

Critics of the OFBCI, such as Americans United for Separation of Church and State (AU)—the American Civil Liberties Union (ACLU), and the Freedom from Religion Foundation (FFRF)—maintain that such a government office, with its policy of awarding government funds to religious organizations, violates the constitutional provision for separation of church and state.

The word church refers to any religious affiliation or activity, and the word state refers to local, state, or federal governments. The phrase "separation of church and state" is not found in the U.S. Constitution, but it refers to the practice of keeping religion and government from unduly influencing one another—a principle that the men who authored the Constitution considered vital to the concept of freedom of religion. For example, because of the "religion clauses" written into the First Amendment, the first of ten amendments called the Bill of Rights, the U.S. government cannot harass Americans who practice their religion, and it cannot declare any religion the "state" religion and demand that citizens worship accordingly, as in centuries past when people could be jailed or otherwise punished for their religious beliefs. Conversely religion is not allowed to dictate certain political or legal decisions, such as determining that a portion of public tax monies be given to specific religions or requiring that elected officials take a religious oath or practice a certain faith in order to assume office.

In addition to protections for freedom of speech, the press, the right of the people "peaceably to assemble," and the right to petition the government for a redress of grievances, the First Amendment states, "Congress shall make no law respecting an

establishment of religion, or prohibiting the free exercise thereof."
These two "religion clauses," called the "establishment clause" and
the "exercise clause," have led to many interpretations on both sides
of the separation of church and state issue.

Because the U.S. Constitution mandates separation of church
and state, when the Office of Faith-Based and Community Initiatives was established, certain restrictions were placed on faith-based
organizations. These included:

- Faith-based organizations could not use government
  funds to support religious activities, such as prayer,
  worship, religious instruction, or sermonizing to
  promote a religion.
- Services receiving government financing could not be
  combined in time or location with religious services.
- Faith-based organizations receiving government funds
  for community assistance could not discriminate on
  the basis of religion. That is, one religion, such as
  Christianity, could not be favored over other religions,
  such as Islam, Buddhism, Hinduism, and so on.

Critics of the OFBCI claim that the government doesn't have
any department that adequately scrutinizes the payment of federal
funds to faith-based organizations. Therefore, they maintain, the
OFBCI's activities consistently violate the separation of church and
state as required by the Constitution. Such violations, the argument
goes, are making it more and more difficult to keep church and
state separate in the United States.

Unlike traditional liberals, during his campaign, President
Barack Obama seized Bush's idea of the faith-based initiative and
converted it into an idea that some liberals could love. Or, some
say, reclaimed it as a Democratic Party initiative, as it had been
in the days of the Reverend Martin Luther King Jr's. civil rights

movement. Obama has called for faith-based programs that can be proven to work, and ways to track whether these faith-based initiatives actually help people, something that wasn't done during the Bush administration. More importantly, Obama sees effective faith-based initiatives as those that help people "of all faiths or no faith at all." Even so, those who believe the state and religion should never meet find nothing but fault with Obama's program.

Separation of church and state has been a concern since the first settlers arrived here, and increasingly after the U.S. Constitution was written. The issue is often in the news during political campaigns, or when courts hand down rulings on a separation of church and state issue that affects many Americans.

Furthermore, the U.S. policy of separation of church and state has made maintaining effective diplomatic relationships with countries that are ruled by religious officials (theocracies) increasingly difficult in the twenty-first century. Some theocracies, notably those in the Middle East, allegedly support terrorist groups whose members commit violent acts that are largely dictated by their religious beliefs. The United States has had to defend itself militarily against such countries, as in the wars against Afghanistan and Iraq.

Within the United States, separation of church and state issues are sometimes contentious. On one side of the issue are those who have interpreted the Constitution to mean that religion has no place in government. People who hold this opinion are sometimes called secularists, or secular humanists. (The word secular is defined as relating to worldly rather than religious issues.) Secularists believe that the First Amendment prohibits all religious signs, symbols, and activities on government property. This prohibition extends to public schools, the argument claims, because county, state, and federal governments finance public schools. People who take this stance generally have no quarrel with others exercising their religious beliefs, but they hold that such activities should not appear to be sponsored by the government, as they might if the government funds certain religions or if religious activities take place on government property.

The arguments for and against keeping government and religion entirely separate often seem to threaten the core beliefs of both sides. For example, some proponents of separation of church and state maintain that the phrase "under God" should be removed from the Pledge of Allegiance and that the phrase "In God We Trust" should not be included on coins and currency minted by the federal government. In addition, they recommend that prayer be eliminated from all public school activities, including athletic events and commencement exercises, and that student religious organizations should not be allowed to hold meetings in public school buildings. Typically included on this side of the argument is the contention that Christianity is shown a preference when religion intrudes upon matters of state.

On the other side of the separation of church and state issue are those who believe that religion has an important place in government. The rationale for this stance is usually that freely held and expressed religious beliefs will enable politicians, officeholders, and others who work within government to make decisions that are more in line with the Christian morals and family values of the general population. The First Amendment was not meant to establish a complete separation of church and state, this side points out, but only to ensure that the government could never designate and fund a state religion. Accordingly, the argument continues, prayer, religious displays, and other religious activities should be allowed in public schools and on government property, as part of the constitutionally guaranteed freedom to exercise one's religion. If allowed, however, the question arises, which religions should be represented, since Americans practice a wide variety of faiths?

People who believe religion has a rightful place in government may also claim that the Declaration of Independence set a precedent (a pattern or a basis in law) for religion in government by using religious phrases such as "endowed by their Creator," "the laws of nature and of nature's God," and "the Supreme Judge of the world." The fact remains, however, that the Declaration of Independence was never a governing document as the U.S. Constitution is.

The two sides of the separation of church and state argument are most often not absolute. That is, some people may argue against religious involvement in government affairs, but condone prayer in schools, printing "In God We Trust" on coins and currency, and including "under God" in the Pledge of Allegiance. Along the same lines, some people may believe that religion has an important role to play in providing moral guidance for individuals as they participate in government affairs, but still be opposed to religious celebrations and displays in schools, oaths of office that affirm a belief in God, or displaying the Ten Commandments in government buildings.

It is useful to learn about separation of church and state issues, because they are often in the news—especially during political campaigns—and because individuals who know all aspects of the argument are better able to make informed decisions. Making informed decisions is important when a person is called upon to vote for candidates for federal and state offices who take a stance on the separation of church and state. Furthermore, since the issue frequently seems to threaten long-held beliefs and opinions, it's important to have an intelligent, considered, and rational discourse to learn what drives the opposite side's argument.

1 The Constitution and Freedom of Religion

THE PHRASE FREEDOM OF RELIGION REFERS TO A government's tolerance for its citizens' religious beliefs. It means that a government will not force its citizens to follow a state-designated religion, and will not discriminate against individuals of any religion or those who have no religion. *Freedom of worship* refers to government tolerance for the actions of individual citizens as they practice their religions, such as praying, worshipping at a designated place, observing certain religious customs, and so on. Freedom of worship, however, does not extend to any activities that harm others, such as human sacrifice.

It's an often-repeated fact of history that many of the first settlers who came to America did so seeking freedom of religion, because many of these immigrants—Catholics, Jews, and Protestants of many denominations, including Puritans—had been living under oppressive governments that sponsored state religions and persecuted those who practiced other religions.

But the colonists themselves were not always tolerant of religious beliefs other than their own. Most agreed that, in matters of social policy, the only correct view was the Christian point of view. Those who did not agree with the predominant view were often severely punished. They could be fined, stripped of personal belongings or land, ostracized, banished from the settlement, jailed, beaten and otherwise tortured, or even killed.

A SCOLD GAGGED.

Though many came to the shores of North America seeking religious freedom, those who found it did not always extend it to others. In this wood engraving of colonial times, an outspoken woman is gagged by Puritans.

For example, Anne Hutchinson, married to merchant William Hutchinson, migrated with her husband and children from England to the Massachusetts Bay Colony in 1634. Hutchinson, an educated woman for her time, soon organized groups to discuss recent church sermons and her own religious views. Pastors and magistrates (local government officials) began to attend Hutchinson's sessions, and they strongly disagreed with many of her beliefs. People did not need ministers to communicate with God, Hutchinson believed, and God's promise of forgiveness alone could gain a sinner admission to heaven. Hutchinson's actions risked her freedom, because all ministers at that time were men, and women were not allowed to preach in public. Furthermore, magistrates used the Bible as their source of law, and they were intolerant of anyone who did not believe in a strict interpretation of its words.

Anne Hutchinson was arrested in 1637 and tried in a Massachusetts Bay Colony court for her views. Governor John Winthrop presided over Hutchinson's trial. In his opening remarks, Winthrop said, "Mrs. Hutchinson, you are called here as one of those that have troubled the peace of the commonwealth and the churches here."

Hutchinson had no lawyer to represent her in court, and she faced a panel of forty-nine men who accused her of eighty-two unlawful acts, including sedition or trying to overthrow the government, voicing opinions that were offensive to God, and overstepping her place as a woman. The panel found Hutchinson guilty and banished her from the Massachusetts Bay Colony. She left in the spring of 1638, and eventually found her way to Providence, in Rhode Island Colony.

At about the same time, Roger Williams was also angering the religious-political leaders of the Massachusetts Bay Colony. Williams first arrived in the colony in 1631, and shortly afterward he turned down an offer from the Boston congregation to serve as a minister because the church had not renounced its ties to the Church of England. Williams, like Hutchinson, was a Puritan who believed that the Church of England was not a true Christian church because it had not been "purified" of worldly ceremonies and institutions. Williams continued to disturb Governor Winthrop and other leaders of the Massachusetts Bay Colony with his admonition that Puritans must expressly separate from the Church of England and his insistence that the land the settlers inhabited should be purchased, rather than simply taken, from the Native Americans who actually owned it. Williams was banished from the colony in 1635. Before he could be deported to England, however, he fled to the area that in 1636 would become Rhode Island Colony. Here he founded Providence—on land that he bought from the Native Americans—and he welcomed others who had fled religious persecution.

Incidents of religious persecution continued throughout many of the thirteen colonies, which were Connecticut, Delaware, Georgia, Maryland, Massachusetts, New Hampshire, New Jersey, New York, North and South Carolina, Pennsylvania, Virginia, and Rhode Island. In many cases, Quakers were singled out for harsh punishment, primarily because their religion was vastly different from other Protestant faiths. The Quakers, also known as the Society of Friends, held to no specific creed. They had no professional clergy and no sacraments of liturgy, since their faith emphasized the inner relationship of a person with God, rather than outward manifestations of Christianity. The Quaker religion forbade its followers to swear oaths to the government or serve in the military, and for this reason, followers of other religions often suspected Quakers of sedition and cowardice.

Some colonies enacted anti-Quaker laws that enabled authorities to banish Quakers. Sometimes the "crime" of being a Quaker was also punishable by whipping, mutilation, or death. Mary Dyer, for example, was a Quaker woman who supported Anne Hutchinson's theology. Dyer was arrested three times and banished from Massachusetts for her religious beliefs. She returned to Massachusetts a fourth time, and in 1660 she was hanged for spreading the Quaker philosophy. (Two other Quakers were also hanged for their religious beliefs in Boston, Massachusetts, during this period.)

Despite evidence of religious persecution in the New World,

immigrants seeking a better life continued to arrive in America. By 1700 the population in the northeastern United States had reached 250,000, with Boston, Massachusetts, the largest city (7,000) and New York City the second largest (5,000). Population increases meant more trade and commerce, which, in turn, meant establishing governments to levy taxes and enforce regulations. The American colonies were still under British rule, and from 1620 to 1700 ruling British monarchs appointed a series of governors to rule the settlements. Many colonists became increasingly unhappy with British rule in the 1700s, citing taxation without representation, repressive laws, and other practices designed to further Britain's interests while disregarding the welfare of colonial settlers.

While Britain remained the governing nation, colonial settlements could obtain a charter from Britain allowing them to form their own local governments. The first town government in the colonies was organized in Dorchester, Massachusetts, in 1633. Local governments passed laws pertaining to business activities, payment of debts, the mandated observance of Sunday as a holy day, and other matters related to the daily lives of settlers within the colonies. Local governments could also restrict religious freedom at will. Such local laws were allowed to stand as long as they did not conflict with British law.

In 1689 Britain passed the Toleration Act, which mandated toleration of all Protestants who swore an oath of allegiance to the English monarchy and rejected the doctrine of transubstantiation. (Transubstantiation refers to the Roman Catholic and Eastern Orthodox doctrine that the bread and wine of communion become, in substance, but not appearance, the actual body and blood of Jesus Christ at consecration.) The Toleration Act applied to all the colonies as well as to Britain, which meant that civil and religious societies in the colonies were assumed to be Protestant.

During the eighteenth century, many people in Germany, France, Britain, and other European countries practiced a philosophy that valued reason, rationality, and scientific proof over the more otherworldly aspects of religion. This intellectual movement, predominant first in Europe and then in the American colonies, was called the Age of Enlightenment.

As the Age of Enlightenment influenced society both in Europe and in the American colonies, religious fervor declined. Then, during the mid-eighteenth century (approximately 1730–1760), the First Great Awakening swept across Europe and the colonies. This movement ushered in a new age of faith to counter the intellectualizing forces that had gained influence during the Age of Enlightenment. To be truly religious, Great Awakening leaders proclaimed, one must trust the heart rather than the head, prize feeling over thinking, and rely on the Bible's teachings rather than human reason.

The American phase of the Great Awakening began among Presbyterians in Pennsylvania and New Jersey. William Tennent, who arrived in the colonies in 1718, and his four sons, all Scotch-Irish Presbyterian ministers, led revivalist meetings in Pennsylvania, exhorting Christians to repent their sinful ways and spread the word of God. Tennent also established a school for clergy called the Log College, known today as Princeton University.

Jonathan Edwards, a well-educated Congregationalist minister who lived in Northampton, Massachusetts, was also a prominent figure in the Great Awakening. In his famous sermon, "Sinners in the Hands of an Angry God," delivered in Enfield, Massachusetts, in 1741, Edwards invoked the image of sinners as spiders, suspended by thin filaments over a fiery hell that he said awaits all those who fail to repent.

The emotional sermons of George Whitefield, an English minister visiting the colonies from Britain, were also influential during the Great Awakening. He inspired many listeners to convert to the Protestant faith and accept Jesus Christ as their personal savior. "Faith is the only wedding garment Christ requires,"

Whitefield told listeners. "He does not call you because you are already, but because he intends to make you Saints."

Inspired by evangelical ministers such as Edwards, Tennent, and Whitefield, itinerant preachers traveled throughout the colonies preaching their fire-and-brimstone versions of the gospel to congregations at revivalist meetings. The ranks of traveling preachers even included a few women and African Americans, and many were moved to serve as missionaries to the southern colonies.

Critics deplored the emotionalism as hundreds of loud, enthusiastic conversions occurred from "the heart," rather than "from the head." Still the number of converts continued to increase.

Although the Great Awakening took place over a short period, it had a lasting effect on early American society. In *Please Don't Wish Me a Merry Christmas: A Critical History of the Separation of Church and State*, author Stephen M. Feldman quotes American historian Richard L. Bushman on the effects of the Great Awakening on colonial America:

> [Between just 1740 and 1743] thousands were converted. People from all ranks of society, of all ages, and from every section underwent the new birth. In New England virtually every congregation was touched. It was not uncommon for ten or twenty percent of a town, having experienced grace, to join the church in a single year. . . . It is safe to say that most of the colonists in the 1740s, if not converted themselves, knew someone who was, or at least heard revival preaching.

Historians have suggested that the eighteenth century's Great Awakening helped prepare American colonists for the challenges they faced as they sought to separate from Britain's rule. Some of those who converted to a more evangelical version of the Christian faith, for example, challenged their local clergy to become more

In the 1908 presidential election, supporters of candidate William Jennings Bryan, who was an evangelical Christian, attacked his opponent William Howard Taft, a Unitarian, calling him "an apostate." (An apostate is one who abandons his faith, cause, or principles.) Taft was elected the nation's twenty-seventh president and was the only president to serve as the U.S. Supreme Court's chief justice after he left office.

Though evangelical Christian William Jennings Bryan's invocation of a "Cross of Gold" won him the Democratic nomination in 1896, he failed to conquer the presidency.

History has shown that when candidates run for president, religion frequently enters the debate:

- William McKinley argued that he was a better Protestant than his opponent for president, William Jennings Bryan.
- Theodore Roosevelt said that the president should attend church regularly, in order to serve as an example to others.
- In the early 1950s, Dwight Eisenhower assured American voters that belief in God was the first principle of Americanism.
- John F. Kennedy, a Catholic, assured voters that if elected president he would not do the Pope's bidding.
- President George W. Bush frequently referred to his faith in public.
- As a candidate, President Obama made it clear that his faith was important to him.

Once elected, U.S. presidents and other elected officials continue to face situations that require them to either reaffirm their own religious convictions or resist pressure to give Christianity more of a voice in government.

For instance, in 1808, Jacob Henry, a Jewish American, won election to North Carolina's state legislature. State requirements for office, however, prevented Henry from being seated unless he became a Protestant and unless he would concede the divine authority of the New Testament. Jews follow the Old Testament and don't believe in the New Testament. Henry risked expulsion from office when he refused to take his oath of office on the New Testament. He delivered a speech saying, "Governments only concern the actions and conduct of man, and not his speculative notions. Who among us feels himself so exalted above his fellows as to have a right to dictate to them any mode of belief?" Henry was allowed to take his seat in the North Carolina state legislature.

Andrew Jackson, the nation's seventh president, resisted the political pressure to form a Christian Party in politics.

Abraham Lincoln, the country's sixteenth president, did not

support a proposal to amend the Preamble to the U.S. Constitution, but neither did Congress or any of the states. The Preamble, as it was originally written, said: "We the people of the United States, in order to form a more perfect union, establish justice, insure domestic tranquility, provide for the common defense, promote the general welfare, and secure the blessings of liberty to ourselves and our posterity, do ordain and establish this Constitution for the United States of America."

The suggested amendments to the Preamble were (proposed changes are italicized):

> We, the people of the United States, *humbly acknowledging almighty God as the source of all authority and power in civil government, the Lord Jesus Christ as the ruler among nations, his revealed will as the supreme law of the land,* in order to constitute a Christian government, and in order to form a more perfect union, establish justice, insure domestic tranquility, provide for the common defense, promote the general welfare, and secure *the inalienable rights* and the blessings of *life,* liberty, *and the pursuit of happiness* to ourselves, our posterity, *and all the people,* do ordain and establish this Constitution for the United States of America.

Just as some Christians sought to bring religion into the Constitution through changes in the Preamble, those on the other side of the separation of church and state argument sought to keep religion out of government. In the 1870s and 1880s, anti-Christians who called themselves "secularists" and "liberals" organized a national campaign to obtain a constitutional amendment guaranteeing separation of church and state. Such amendments found little support in Congress or among the general population and were not passed. A leader in the effort, Francis Ellingwood Abbot, however, founded a newspaper called the *Index* in 1870 that provided a forum for liberal views about the separation of church and state.

Abbot coined the term *liberalism*, hoping that his allies would adopt it and unite under his leadership to become a politically effective group dedicated to the separation of church and state. In pursuit of this goal, in 1872 Abbot published his "Nine Demands of Liberalism," asking that "our entire political system shall be founded and administered on a purely secular basis." The "Demands" also specified:

1. Church property should no longer be exempt from taxation.

2. Chaplains in Congress, state legislatures, the military, and in prisons and other public institutions should no longer be employed by the government and paid with public funds.

3. Public funds should no longer be used for religious education or charitable institutions.

4. The use of the Bible in public schools should be prohibited.

5. The president of the United States and all state governors should be prohibited from issuing proclamations for religious "festivals and fasts."

6. The judicial oath in courts and other government departments that contain the phrase "under God" should be exchanged for simple affirmations "under the pains and penalties of perjury."

7. All laws enforcing the observance of Sunday as the Sabbath should be repealed.

8. All laws should be structured to conform to rules of morality, equal rights, and liberty for all, rather than to "Christian" morality.

9. There should be no privilege or advantage to Christianity or any other religion in the U.S. Constitution and in state constitutions.

Abbot and his liberal followers did not succeed in changing the law or the Constitution with their list of demands. However, the debate concerning possible amendments to the constitution that would either strengthen or weaken the wall of separation between church and state has continued.

Not only do presidents freely invoke God in public speeches, but it has become common practice for political candidates to discuss religion—both their own and their opponents'—during campaigns. How do voters feel about the practice? A Gallup Poll conducted in 2007 found Americans almost evenly divided on the question "Do you think it's appropriate for candidates to talk about their religious beliefs during their political campaigns?" Fifty percent of those polled said yes, it was appropriate, and 48 percent said no, it was not. However, because America is largely a religious country and many voters associate religion with morals and values, Americans often question political candidates about their religious beliefs.

In the campaign for the 2008 presidential election, for example, candidates of both political parties rushed to assure voters of their belief in God and "family values." Republican presidential candidate Mitt Romney, a former governor of Massachusetts and a devout Mormon, was uniquely challenged during the 2008 campaign. (*Mormon* is the shortened term used to refer to members of the Church of Jesus Christ of Latter-Day Saints.) Not only did he have to convince voters of his ability to lead the country, but he also had to assure them that Mormonism is not a heretical cult, as some Christians apparently believed. "My view is that when a person of faith is running for office—particularly a faith you may not be familiar with—there are some questions that are legitimate," Romney told a writer for *Newsweek* in December 2007. Legitimate questions for voters to ask, Romney summarized, included: Would authorities of the candidate's church influence his decisions when he took office? Could a president of faith put America's traditions and laws above those of his church? Voters could rightfully expect a candidate to address those issues, Romney said, but other "theological concepts" did not need to be explained, regardless of one's faith.

Mike Huckabee, another candidate for the Republican nomination for president in the 2008 election, is an ordained Southern Baptist minister and former governor of Arkansas. He was also challenged during his campaign to defend his faith without criticizing other faiths. As the campaign was heating up in late 2007, reporters asked Huckabee what he thought of a speech Romney had delivered, in which he vowed to serve the interests of the United States over the interests of the Mormon Church. Huckabee replied, "I think it's a good thing and healthy for all of us . . . to discuss faith in the public square." But when asked if he thought women should be ordained as ministers, a topic of concern to Southern Baptists, Huckabee declined to express his opinion. "It's so irrelevant to being president that I wouldn't even get into that," Huckabee said. Throughout the early days of the campaign, Huckabee consistently refused to discuss the details of his own religious beliefs, beyond saying that he believed in God, Jesus, and the importance of values to the office of president.

A question posed to the nine Republican candidates for president during their first public debate on May 3, 2007, broadcast on television and over the Internet, startled some viewers. A Politico. com (a political news website) reader submitted the question, "Do you believe in evolution?" Senator John McCain, who eventually secured the Republican nomination for president in the 2008 election, answered "yes," with the caveat, "But I also believe, when I hike the Grand Canyon and see it at sunset, that the hand of God is there also." Before the other eight candidates could answer the question, the debate moderator asked, "I'm curious, is there anybody on the stage that does not believe in evolution?" Three candidates—Senator Sam Brownback (Kansas), Mike Huckabee (former Arkansas governor), and Representative Tom Tancredo (Colorado)—raised their hands. The debate moderator then moved on to another question, effectively closing the evolution discussion. Since Brownback, Huckabee, and Tancredo soon fell far behind McCain both in raising campaign funds and winning the support of influential Republicans, it would seem that most Americans watching the campaign were more moderate than extremist in their views toward political candidates' religious beliefs. Some debate viewers barely noticed the question or the responses, while others were shocked and concerned. Shouldn't presidential hopefuls recognize evolution as a scientific fact, these viewers asked? Perhaps more to the point, if one hopes to become the nation's commander in chief who, if elected, promises to "preserve, protect, and defend" the U.S. Constitution, should he or she be required to answer such a question? That is, doesn't the question itself become questionable, many viewers wondered after the debate, since it could be construed as a violation of the constitutional prohibition against religious tests for public office?

The often controversial but familiar mix of religion and politics ignited a political and media firestorm in 2008, when President Barack Obama, then a Democratic senator from Illinois, and the Democratic presidential candidate, was criticized for his relationship with the Reverend Jeremiah Wright, whom he had once called his "spiritual advisor." Wright had come under fire for sermons that placed the blame for the September 11, 2001, terrorist attacks on the U.S. government. Wright compared American soldiers to the Roman legions that executed Christ, saying that the government itself was practicing terrorism, and suggested that the AIDS epidemic was a racist plot against African Americans.

Fearing that his association with Wright would hinder his chances of being elected, Obama sought to distance himself from his former pastor. During an April 2008 speech at the National Press Club in Washington, D.C., Obama accused Wright of "insensitivity" and "outrageousness." "He does not speak for me," Obama continued. "He does not speak for the campaign and so he may make statements in the future that don't reflect my values or concerns." Although his rival for the presidency tried to use his past affiliation with Wright to scare people away from voting for Obama, it did not work.

The fear that religion might have too much influence in the nation's public life has not been shared by all Americans, but was obviously prevalent in the latter years of the twentieth century. However, as Stephen L. Carter points out in *God's Name in Vain: The Wrongs and Rights of Religion in Politics*, the attitude that religion should have no place in politics would have put an end to the nineteenth-century abolition movement, which was led by Christian evangelicals who were mostly clergy and preached fiery sermons about a Christian's duty to love his neighbor as himself. Slavery was against the teachings of the Bible, the abolitionists preached, and it was God's will for it to be abolished, regardless of the cost to slaveholders in the South. Furthermore, in the early twentieth century, when the industrial age was in full swing, men, women, and children worked at dangerous jobs for pennies a day and could be fired, beaten, arrested, and even murdered for trying to form unions. As Carter explains, religious people were among those who spoke out strongly against the widespread abuse of workers in the name of corporate profit and also helped bring about social change that included the push for public education, the battle for women's rights, the improvement of prisons and hospitals, and various crusades for world peace.

Many advocates for social change did not concern themselves with confining their views about justice or the fair and decent treatment of American citizens to a narrow, separate area called "religion." The Reverend Martin Luther King Jr., for example, based his outspoken leadership of the civil rights movement in the mid-1960s on his religious beliefs, but his concern was for society's treatment of minorities in America. Human rights need not be confirmed by the state, he often argued, but were "God given."

King worked for social change—an end to segregation in the United States—but he did it through the democratic process, and not through violence. "Let us march on ballot boxes," he said at the conclusion of the famous march from Selma to Montgomery, Alabama, in 1965, "until we send to our city councils, state legislatures, and the U.S. Congress, men who will not fear to do justice, love mercy, and walk humbly with their God."

Clearly, religion and politics have long intermingled, and the mix will continue to raise questions about religion's influence on public policy. One side of the debate that is seldom considered, however, is the argument for keeping a distance between religion and politics for the sake of freedom of religion. Carter writes in *The Culture of Disbelief: How American Law and Politics Trivialize Religious Devotion* that the major religions practiced in the United States—mainstream Protestantism, Catholicism, and Judaism—generally receive adequate protection under the law. However, he adds, "Religions that most need protection seem to receive it least." American Indians, for instance, have seen their sacred lands taken for roads to facilitate logging and have been denied the use of peyote in their religious rituals because of anti-drug laws. "Imagine the brouhaha," Carter says, "if New York City were to try to take St. Patrick's Cathedral by eminent domain to build a new convention center."

"The problem goes well beyond our society's treatment of those who simply want freedom to worship in ways that most Americans find troubling," Carter continues. "An analogous difficulty is posed by those whose religious convictions move them to action in the public arena." For example, when people who believe that God's will requires them to oppose abortion make their opposition known, others may complain that they are trying to impose their religious views on them. Furthermore, if the Supreme Court were to rule that abortion is illegal in the United States, many citizens would complain that religion had held too much sway over politics and had unduly influenced the Court's decision.

Martin Luther King Jr.
A Chronology

- He was born January 15, 1929, in Atlanta, Georgia
- In 1944, he graduated from high school at the age of fifteen.
- In 1948, he received a bachelor's degree from Morehouse College in Atlanta.
- In 1951, he received a degree in theology from Crozer Theological Seminary in Chester, Pennsylvania.
- In 1953, he received a Ph.D. from Boston University.
- In 1955–1956, he gained national prominence for his role in the Montgomery (Alabama) bus boycott.
- In 1957, King helped found the Southern Christian Leadership Conference, which was instrumental in the civil rights movement.
- In 1964, at the age of thirty-five, he was the youngest person ever to receive the Nobel Peace Prize.
- On April 4, 1968, Martin Luther King was assassinated while standing on the balcony of his motel room in Memphis, Tennessee, where he was to lead a protest march in sympathy with city sanitation workers.
- James Earl Ray, a petty criminal who had escaped from jail a year earlier, confessed to King's murder in 1969. He pled guilty in court, but recanted his confession and protested his innocence until his death in prison in 1998.
- In 1997, Ray met with Dexter King, Martin Luther King's son. "I had nothing to do with shooting your father," Ray told King. The King family believed Ray, but the case was never tried and the verdict was never overturned.

hopelessly flawed. They favor large, well-established, high or formal churches and discriminate against small, new, unconventional, informal or low churches."

The question "What constitutes a religion?" has been answered in court, and since court decisions set precedent for future lawsuits, court-determined definitions of religion are reliable guidelines. When laws are interpreted in courts, the prevailing judgment has been that, although a law may restrict some aspect of a religion, it is allowed to stand if the law is for the greater good.

For example, in 1899, the Supreme Court ruled that awarding a federal grant to a Roman Catholic organization for construction of a hospital did not violate the First Amendment, since people of all faiths would benefit. Similarly, in 1947, in *Everson* v. *Board of Education*, the Court reviewed the rights of local school districts to provide free bus transportation to children attending parochial (religious) schools. After all arguments were heard, the Court allowed the provision of transportation, determining that the bus transportation was a form of "public welfare legislation" that was being extended "to all its citizens without regard to their religious belief." However, Justice Hugo Black, who wrote the Court's opinion, also recognized that "it approaches the verge" of the State's constitutional power. The Court held:

> The "establishment of religion" clause of the First Amend-
> ment means at least this: Neither a state nor the Federal
> Government can set up a church. Neither can pass laws
> which aid one religion, aid all religions, or prefer one
> religion over another. Neither can force nor influence a
> person to go to or to remain away from church against
> his will or force him to profess a belief or disbelief in any
> religion. No person can be punished for entertaining
> or professing religious beliefs or disbeliefs, for church
> attendance or non-attendance. No tax in any amount,

large or small, can be levied to support any religious activities or institutions, whatever they may be called, or whatever form they may adopt to teach or practice religion. Neither a state nor the Federal Government can, openly or secretly, participate in the affairs of any religious organizations or groups and vice versa. In the words of Jefferson, the clause against establishment of religion by law was intended to erect "a wall of separation" between church and State. . . . [The First] Amendment requires the state to be a neutral in its relations with groups of religious believers and non believers; it does not require the state to be their adversary. State power is no more to be used so as to handicap religions than it is to favor them.

Many landmark court cases concerning religious freedom and separation of church and state have reached the U.S. Supreme Court, where nine justices usually decide matters involving the U.S. Constitution. Cases typically reach the Supreme Court only after decisions are handed down in lower courts and either the plaintiffs or defendants appeal the decision. The Supreme Court justices decide which cases they will hear. Since the Supreme Court is the highest court in the nation, its decisions are final, although it may decide to return a case to a lower court for another hearing.

In 1971, in *Lemon* v. *Kurtzman*, the Supreme Court's decision was important because it established a three-part test that became the standard for establishment-clause cases that followed. In deciding whether or not a state or federal law violated the establishment clause, the justices in this case focused on three points: sponsorship, financial support, and active involvement of the government in a religious activity. Under this test, a law would be constitutional only if it had a "secular purpose" (a purpose that is not religious), a "primary effect" that neither advances nor inhibits religion, and if it does not create an "excessive government entanglement" with religion.

Applying this test, the justices in *Lemon* decided that a Pennsylvania law that allowed the state superintendent of public instruction to reimburse nonpublic schools, most of which were Catholic, for teachers' salaries, textbooks, and other instructional materials violated the establishment clause and was, therefore, unconstitutional.

The Supreme Court again applied the test devised in *Lemon* in a 1973 decision. In 1969 Frederick Walz, a property owner in Richmond County, New York, challenged New York's property-tax exemptions for religious organizations on the grounds that such exemptions forced him, through his tax dollars, to contribute to religious organizations. In 1970, the Supreme Court held its decision on this case, *Walz* v. *Tax Commission of City of New York*, that New York's property tax exemptions for religious organizations were not unconstitutional. The Court noted that tax exemptions for churches and other religious organizations were not required by the First Amendment's establishment clause, but such exemptions are "deeply embedded in the fabric of our national life."

Furthermore, the Court ruled that the New York legislature had a "secular legislative purpose" in granting the exemption, because it had "not singled out one particular church or religious group or even churches as such." Instead the exemption was granted "to all houses of religious worship within a broad class of property owned by nonprofit, quasi-public corporations which include hospitals, libraries, playgrounds, scientific, professional, historical, and patriotic groups." Also in line with the *Lemon* test, the exemption helped prevent government "entanglement" with religious groups.

In later decisions, the Supreme Court seemed increasingly willing to accommodate religion. For example, in *Marsh* v. *Chambers*, decided in 1983, the Court abandoned the tests used in *Lemon*, relying instead on historical custom when it upheld the widespread practice of saying prayers at the opening of state legislative sessions. Ernest Chambers, a Nebraska state legislator, had

How Presidents Influence the Supreme Court

Since Supreme Court justices serve on the court for life, presidents are not often called upon to nominate a justice to replace one of the nine on the bench. Such job security within the government is reserved only for Supreme Court justices, to help ensure their independence from Congress and the president. Nominating a Supreme Court justice is one of the president's most important duties.

Article II, Section 2, clause 2 of the Constitution says that the president "shall nominate, and by and with the Advice and Consent of the Senate, shall appoint . . . Judges of the Supreme Court." Once the Senate confirms the president's choice, the new justice is appointed. The president generally nominates a person he believes will decide cases in ways that agree with his administration's policies. For example, a liberal president may hope that Supreme Court decisions will reflect his strict separation of church and state views, while a conservative president may hope to see the justices lean toward allowing some interplay between church and state.

When the political views of the president and the majority of the Senate differ greatly, appointing a new justice to the Supreme Court can be a difficult and lengthy process. Excellence and professionalism are the preferred qualities in nominees, but politics also influences the process. Between the appointment of the first justices in 1789 and 2006, the Senate confirmed 120 of the 154 nominated Supreme Court justices.

brought suit against the practice, on the grounds that it constituted an establishment of religion. The Supreme Court's decision was that such practices are not unconstitutional, based on the fact that the practice has become "part of the fabric of our society." "It is," wrote Chief Justice Warren Burger, "simply a tolerable acknowledgment of beliefs widely held among the people of this country."

Supreme Court decisions reflect, to some extent, how many justices are liberal in their views and how many are conservative. In church versus state issues, a majority of liberal justices may mean that decisions most often reflect a strict separation of church versus state, while if the majority of justices are conservative, decisions could lean more toward allowing less separation.

For example, in *Lynch* v. *Donnelly*, the court ruled on the constitutionality of Pawtucket, Rhode Island's decision to include a nativity scene in its Christmas display in a shopping district. In addition to the nativity scene, the display included a Santa Claus house, a Christmas tree, and a banner wishing shoppers "Season's Greetings." Daniel Donnelly, a resident of Pawtucket, objected to the nativity scene being displayed on city property and filed suit against Pawtucket's mayor, Dennis Lynch. The Court held that, although the nativity scene had religious significance, the city was not attempting to establish a state church, and, therefore, had not violated the establishment clause. In writing the Court's majority opinion, Chief Justice Burger pointed out that it was "far too late in the day to impose a crabbed reading of the [establishment] Clause on the country."

In addition to precedent-setting decisions concerning the establishment clause, the First Amendment's free exercise clause has also frequently been debated in the Supreme Court.

In 1940, in *Cantwell* v. *Connecticut*, the Supreme Court debated a case involving a Connecticut man, Newton Cantwell, and his two sons, Jesse and Russell, who were Jehovah's Witnesses. As required by their religion, the Cantwells were approaching people on the street in a Catholic neighborhood to preach their religion and going door-to-door to distribute religious literature. Two pedestrians voluntarily listened to an anti-Roman Catholic recording on the Cantwells' portable phonograph, then angrily reported the Cantwells to city authorities. The Cantwells were subsequently arrested for inciting a breach of the peace and for failing to acquire a permit required for solicitation. The Cantwells countercharged that the breach of peace and solicitation ordinances violated their free speech and freedom of religion rights. The case eventually reached the U.S. Supreme Court.

In a unanimous decision, the Court ruled in favor of the Cantwells. The Court held that although general regulations on solicitation were legal, regulations that banned solicitation on religious grounds were not. The decision also emphasized that the First Amendment embraces two concepts—the freedom to believe as one chooses and the freedom to act, as long as the resultant actions are not a threat to society. While the Cantwell's message might be offensive to some people, it did not threaten bodily harm and therefore was constitutionally protected religious speech.

In *Sherbert* v. *Verner*, argued in 1963, the Court sought to address the question of what types of religious actions would be allowed under the free-exercise clause. Adeil Sherbert, a member of the Seventh-day Adventist Church, was fired from her job in a textile mill when she refused to work on Saturday, her religious Sabbath observance day. The South Carolina Employment Security Commission refused to accept Sherbert's religious reasons for her refusal to work on Saturdays, and denied her unemployment compensation. The Supreme Court held that the South Carolina Employment Security Commission had violated Sherbert's First and Fourteenth Amendment rights, since the state's eligibility requirements for unemployment compensation placed a burden on Sherbert's ability to freely exercise her faith, and there was no compelling state interest to justify the burden. Therefore, Sherbert

property at government-sponsored events and, as a result, were not private speech, but public speech, and were, therefore, a violation of the First Amendment's establishment clause.

Supreme Court decisions have set important precedents for lower courts to follow when judging public school/religion cases, and have provided guidelines for public school districts when considering whether or not to allow prayer and other forms of worship at school functions. They have not, however, resolved the argument in the minds of those parents, educators, students, and others who feel strongly about the issue.

Those who oppose prayer and other religious activities in public schools maintain that proponents have confused the state's neutral stance with hostility. Religion or lack of religion is a private matter, this side argues, and its instruction and practice should be left to parents in the privacy of their homes or in their places of worship. Others decry the absence of prayer in public schools and argue that the Supreme Court has taken too hard a stance against the freedom of public school students to pray when and how they want.

Prayer is not the only separation of church and state issue affecting the American public school system. Christians' criticism of public schools centers on the charges that they promote anti-Christian values and that they prevent parents from teaching their children values based on religion. For instance, those Christians who believe the Bible to be true in all respects object to the public schools' choice to teach evolution in science classes. Others believe that abstaining from sexual activity should be the only choice as their children mature sexually, and they object to schools' attempts to teach safe-sex practices that involve the use of condoms and birth control pills. Some people do not want other religions taught as equal to Christianity, and some don't want alternative families, such as gay and lesbian households, to be mentioned in classrooms at all. For nearly every intersection of religion in schools and the law, there are people who object.

Some parents have given up on public schools and choose to educate their children at home or to send them to religious schools. Others have become active in battles to change the public school curricula. The teaching of evolution in science classes is particularly unpopular among those Christians who believe in a literal interpretation of the Bible. The evolution issue was first tackled in court in 1925, in the now-famous *Tennessee* v. *Scopes* trial. Journalists called it "the trial of the century" because it pitted Clarence Darrow and William Jennings Bryan, two famous attorneys of the day, against one another. Newspapers also nicknamed it "the monkey trial," referring to the evolutionary theory that people evolved from apes.

John Thomas Scopes, a teacher in Dayton, Tennessee, was accused of violating a state law against teaching evolution instead of creationism—which the state mandated—in public schools. Local activists had encouraged Scopes to teach evolution as a deliberate test of the constitutionality of the state's anti-evolution law. Scopes's attorney was Clarence Darrow, a successful trial lawyer, an agnostic (one who doubts the existence of God), and a longtime opponent of teaching creationism as fact. Prosecutor William Jennings Bryan, also a well-known attorney and a three-time candidate for president, opposed the teaching of evolution in public schools and believed in a literal interpretation of the Bible.

In the stifling July heat, in Rhea County Courthouse in Dayton, Tennessee, the two attorneys battled. A jury of twelve mostly middle-aged men, consisting of farmers and churchgoers, heard the case. The defense sought not to have Scopes acquitted, but to get a ruling from a higher court, preferably the U.S. Supreme Court, that Tennessee's anti-evolution law was unconstitutional. Darrow was not allowed to pursue this line of defense, so he relied instead on his argument that "civilization" was on trial, against religious zealots who would make the Bible "every man's" last word. Prosecutor Bryan introduced the book of Genesis from the King

William Jennings Bryan fought for the presidency and lost, but he also fought against teaching evolution in the schools in the infamous *Scopes* trial of 1925.

James version of the Bible to bolster his side of the argument. Bryan also took the stand as a witness for the prosecution and an expert on the Bible, stumbling under Darrow's relentless questioning. At one point Bryan answered, "I do not think about things I don't think about." Darrow then asked, "Do you think about things you do think about?" The spectators laughed when Bryan responded, "Well, sometimes."

In his closing speech, Darrow asked the jury to return a guilty verdict against his client, in order to allow an appeal to the Tennessee Supreme Court. The jury complied, and a year later the Tennessee Supreme Court reversed the decision on a technicality, but not on the constitutional grounds for which Darrow had hoped. Five days after the trial was over, William Jennings Bryan died.

In 1925, when the Scopes trial made headlines, fifteen states had passed laws against teaching evolution in public schools. As time passed the laws were seldom enforced, but their constitutionality was not effectively challenged until *Epperson* v. *Arkansas* in 1968.

Susan Epperson, a young woman with a master's degree in zoology, taught high school biology in Little Rock, Arkansas. Epperson was asked to teach from a textbook that included a section on evolution. Since Arkansas still had a 1925 anti-evolution statute on its books, Epperson faced a dilemma. If she taught from the required textbook, she could possibly face criminal charges and dismissal (although Arkansas was not actively enforcing its anti-evolution statute, and probably would not have prosecuted Epperson). To solve her perceived dilemma, Epperson challenged the law in a state court. The court's decision was that Arkansas' anti-evolution law was unconstitutional because it violated the free speech provision of the First Amendment—not the establishment clause, which says the government cannot establish a religion.

Since some parents believed that teaching evolution, which presents theories of the origins of human beings and other species that differ from biblical accounts, was counter to their religious beliefs, they continued to push to include creationism as an alternative to evolution in teaching science. In some areas the push was successful. In 1987, however, the U.S. Supreme Court ruled that states cannot require public schools to balance evolution lessons by teaching creationism.

Science
and
Religion

When the Dover, Pennsylvania, school board decided in October 2004 to require ninth- grade biology students to hear a brief statement at the start of the semester saying that there were "gaps" in the theory of evolution, that intelligent design was an alternative, and that students could learn more about it by reading a textbook, *Of Pandas and People*, available in the high school library, they did not anticipate the furor that the decision would cause. In December 2004, eleven parents, represented by the American Civil Liberties Union (ACLU), Americans United for Separation of Church and State (AU), and a private law firm, Pepper Hamilton LLP, sued the school board, alleging violation of the separation of church and state, since, the group maintained, intelligent design is a religious concept.

As the first school board in the United States to introduce the concept of intelligent design in science classes, the Dover board was the center of national media attention. The trial concluded on November 4, 2005, with the decision that intelligent design is a religious concept, and teaching it in schools violates the establishment clause of the First Amendment.

Also in November 2005, the PBS science program *Nova* presented a documentary on the Dover trial called "Judgment Day: Intelligent Design on Trial." Phillip Johnson, the father of intelligent design, presented his definition of the concept: "There are two hypotheses to consider scientifically. One is you need a creative intelligence to do all the creating that has been done in the history of life; the other is you don't." Neither hypothesis should be taught as absolute scientific fact, Johnson said.

One of the scientists who weighed in on the subject, Ken Miller, a biologist from Brown University in Rhode Island, said that "what science isn't very good at is answering questions [on] the meaning and purpose of things." He said science involves investigation and problem-solving in the material world, using material tools. When the supernatural world is offered as an explanation for occurrences in the material world, however, that's a "science stopper." That is, supernatural explanations for nature prohibit further scientific inquiry.

The 1987 Supreme Court ruling against mandating the teaching of creationism in public school science classes did not permanently settle the issue. In 2005, for example, Christian activists campaigned to have "intelligent design," the theory that some organisms are so complex that natural evolutionary selection cannot alone account for them, taught in science classes as an alternative to evolution. When the Dover, Pennsylvania, school district mandated the teaching of intelligent design in biology classes in October 2004, a group of parents filed suit against the district, alleging that the school district was approving the teaching of religion. U.S. district judge John E. Jones heard the case, *Kitzmiller* v. *Dover School District,* in November 2005, and published his decision a month later.

Judge Jones delivered a stinging opinion against the Dover school district, holding that the district had violated the Constitution's First Amendment. Jones's ruling stated that intelligent design "is a religious view, a mere re-labeling of creationism, and not a scientific theory." Jones also criticized the "breathtaking inanity" of the Dover action and accused several school board members of lying to conceal their true motive, which was to promote religion. The Dover school district members who instituted the measure were voted out of office.

In 2005, when President George W. Bush said that he believed schools should teach both the theories of evolution and intelligent design, those in favor of teaching intelligent design were encouraged. However, after the *Dover* decision, many states issued mandates against teaching intelligent design or creationism in public school science classes, but some state education boards (e.g., Kansas) recommended teaching "doubts" about the certainty of evolution, which supporters praised as "a victory for free speech" and opponents criticized as "shabby politics and worse science."

Although local school boards have the last word in structuring public school curricula, state education boards responsible for student testing influence local decisions: If state tests require students to know certain facts, then local school districts will generally structure curricula to provide those facts, and may decide not to mandate teaching material that could cause the school district to be challenged in court.

As these landmark legal cases show, public schools remain a battlefield where the religious beliefs and values of parents, students, teachers, public school board members, school administrators, and others in the community often clash. The conflicts affect the lives of everyone who is interested in public education and are not likely to end soon.

Woman's Christian Temperance Union (WCTU) joined the ranks of temperance organizations in 1873. WCTU members stood outside saloons singing hymns and reading the Bible. They also preached observance of the Sabbath, and visited prisoners in jail to encourage moral behavior and abstinence from alcohol.

In 1893 members of the WCTU were joined in their fight to abolish alcohol by the all-male members of the Anti-Saloon League, who advocated for the enforcement of existing temperance laws, as well as new legislation to outlaw alcoholic beverages. Under the motto "the saloon must go" members used local churches to carry their temperance message to the people. League members were also committed to supporting political candidates who were "dry" (against the sale of alcohol in their political districts) and opposing "wet" candidates (those who did not oppose the sale of alcohol).

In 1919 the temperance movement culminated in the ratification of the Eighteenth Amendment to the Constitution, which mandated Prohibition, making it illegal to manufacture, transport, and sell alcoholic beverages. Congress passed the Volstead Act in 1919, allowing the government to enforce provisions of the Eighteenth Amendment. Prohibition proved impossible to enforce, however, due to widespread bootlegging (making and selling liquor illegally) and flouting of the law and federal underfunding for enforcement. In fact, organized crime flourished during Prohibition, due to involvement in bootlegging and running "speakeasies" (clandestine bars where liquor was sold illegally). The speakeasies not only promoted drinking, but also gambling, prostitution, and tobacco use. By 1933 the Eighteenth Amendment was considered a lost cause and the Twenty-First Amendment, repealing Prohibition, was passed.

The Prohibition era (1920-1933) ushered in additional laws governing moral behavior. It was illegal to sell cigarettes in some states, and in some locations there was strict local censorship of books, films, plays, and other forms of entertainment. Anti-prostitution laws were already on the books in most communities,

The Eighteenth Amendment, which mandated the prohibition of legal alcohol, was arguably the least popular amendment ever passed. Among the punishments for the possession of alcohol while Prohibition was in effect was to have to dispose of it in the street. If that was done now, the offenders would be arrested again for crimes against the environment!

but after Prohibition ended, they were generally more stridently enforced. (Despite laws against prostitution, however, the practice continues throughout the United States. Nevada is the only state that has legalized prostitution, and in that state prostitutes must be periodically tested for sexually transmitted and other communicable diseases and must pay income taxes.)

Sabbatarian laws, such as the prohibition against retail and alcohol sales on Sunday, remained in effect in many American communities through the twentieth and into the twenty-first centuries, but they were often so honeycombed with exceptions that they were seldom enforced.

The Supreme Court first decided an establishment clause challenge to a Sunday-closing law in 1961, in *McGowan* v. *Maryland*.

In this case, employees of a large department store in Maryland were convicted and fined in a state court for selling certain products on Sunday. The products that the employees were convicted of selling included a loose-leaf binder, a can of floor wax, a stapler, staples, and a toy. This violated a county law that only allowed Sunday sales of tobacco products, candy, milk, bread, fruit, gasoline, oils, greases, drugs, medicines, newspapers, and periodicals. (Later amendments exempted from the law the retail sale in Anne Arundel County of all foodstuffs, automobile and boating accessories, flowers, toilet goods, hospital supplies, and souvenirs. Amendments also exempted entirely any retail establishment in that county that employed not more than one person other than the owner.) The Court noted that there were many other Maryland laws that prohibited specific activities on Sundays or limited them to certain hours, places, or conditions.

The Supreme Court held that the county law under which the department store employees were convicted did not violate the establishment clause of the First Amendment. The decision read, in part:

> In the light of the evolution of our Sunday Closing Laws through the centuries, and of their more or less recent emphasis upon secular considerations, it is concluded that, as presently written and administered, most of them, at least, are of a secular, rather than of a religious, character, and that presently they bear no relationship to establishment of religion, as those words are used in the Constitution of the United States.

In modern times, Sunday closing laws are the norm in some communities, but in most areas they are absent or are not enforced. Modern societal moral issues, and, therefore, legislation and court challenges, center more around abortion, homosexuality and the rights of gays and lesbians, same-sex marriage, and scientific research that involves the use of human embryos or other reproductive tissues. When federal and state governments pass laws regulating these topics, the laws may be challenged as violations of the separation of church and state if people perceive them as based on religious beliefs. The Supreme Court case around which the current controversy over abortion centers is *Roe* v. *Wade*. Since many people oppose abortion on religious grounds, some consider laws that regulate abortion a violation of the separation of church and state.

Roe v. *Wade* involved twenty-one-year-old Norma McCorvey, a Dallas, Texas, resident, who became pregnant in 1969. She was divorced at the time, and her parents were raising her young child. McCorvey was having trouble finding work because of her pregnancy, and she dreaded the stigma attached to an illegitimate birth. She looked for a physician who would perform an abortion, but was unsuccessful, because, at that time, Texas was one of forty-six states that had laws against abortion. The Texas law had been passed in 1859, and was similar to antiabortion laws in other states in that it targeted for prosecution those who performed abortions, not the women who requested them.

During her search for an abortion provider, McCorvey met two attorneys, Sarah Weddington and Linda Coffee, who wanted to challenge the state's antiabortion law, and she agreed to file a lawsuit under the fictitious name "Jane Roe." The class action lawsuit, representing all pregnant women in Texas, was filed against Henry Wade, the district attorney in Dallas County, Texas. The suit alleged that Roe had limited rights to an abortion. It asked the court to find the Texas antiabortion law unconstitutional, and to prevent the state from enforcing it.

On appeal the *Roe* case reached the U.S. Supreme Court, where it was decided in 1973. (In the meantime, Norma McCorvey gave birth, and the child was put up for adoption.) The Court held that the Texas law was unconstitutional, not because it violated

Those who are most fervently antiabortion usually cite religious grounds for their beliefs. The *Roe v. Wade* case, decided by the Supreme Court in 1973, made abortion a legal, private matter. Thirty-six years later, those on either side of the issue are still debating each other in public—and in private.

the separation of church and state, but because of the Fourteenth Amendment's "due process clause." The clause states, in part: "No state shall make or enforce any law which shall abridge the privileges or immunities of citizens of the United States; nor shall any State deprive any person of life, liberty, or property, without due process of law." In short, the Court decided that the Constitution protects privacy, and it should be legal for a woman to make the private decision of whether or not to have an abortion, for any reason, during the first two trimesters (six months) of the pregnancy. States could impose restrictions and regulate abortions after that. (In 2003 Congress passed a law banning "partial birth" abortions in the United States—those that would take place during the second or third trimesters of a pregnancy.)

Precedent for the decision in the Roe case had been established in a 1965 Supreme Court decision in *Griswold* v. *Connecticut.* In this case, the director of the Planned Parenthood League of Connecticut and the League's medical director were convicted of giving birth control information, instruction, and medical advice to married couples, a practice that was against a Catholic-inspired law against birth control in Connecticut and in many other states. The Supreme Court ruled this law unconstitutional under the Ninth Amendment, holding that the amendment established a right to privacy that the Connecticut law violated.

The right to privacy, McCorvey's attorneys successfully argued in *Roe*, also applied to a woman's decision of whether or not to bear a child. The state argued during the case, however, that human life should be protected, and that most religions agreed with that stance. Norma McCorvey revealed her identity in 1995, the same year she converted to Christianity, and she has since proclaimed her support for those who oppose abortion.

The decision in *Roe* v. *Wade* made history, since it made abortion legal in the United States during the first six months of a pregnancy. Since the decision, many states have passed laws that restrict abortion rights. However, ballot initiatives in South Dakota and Colorado that would have stongly restricted abortion rights were soundly defeated in November 2008. In the unlikely event that the Supreme Court ever overturns *Roe* v. *Wade*, some states may immediately enact laws to once again make abortion illegal, while other states may pass laws making abortion legal in that state, regardless of federal law. Since *Roe* v. *Wade*, groups on both sides of the issue have loudly asserted their views. There are two main positions on the pro-life side:

1. Mainstream pro-life advocates believe that abortion should only be legal in cases of rape, incest, or when the pregnancy endangers the mother's life. If *Roe* v. *Wade* should be overturned, it is possible that the mainstream pro-life position would prevail.

2. Absolutist pro-life advocates are more likely to take the position that abortion should never be legal, and individuals on

this side of the issue are sometimes fanatical in their views. For instance, Planned Parenthood facilities—most of which no longer provide abortion services—have frequently been harassed, as antiabortion groups and individuals picket outside their doors and shout curses at women who go there seeking medical advice. In some cases, antiabortion fanatics have bombed offices where they believe abortions take place, resulting in laws that require protesters to stay a certain distance away from the facilities. Lists of physicians suspected of performing abortions, including their addresses, have been posted on the Internet, and some physicians have been injured and even killed.

Evangelicals and traditional Catholics generally take the pro-life side of the abortion issue, arguing that taking a human life is never defensible. Most people of faith, however, do not condone the hate and violence that the abortion issue sometimes inspires.

The pro-choice side of the abortion issue holds that a woman should have free choice over whether or not to bear a child, regardless of the circumstances of conception.

Other moral issues concerning society in the twenty-first century include whether or not homosexuals should have the right to marry, plus all the legal rights that marriage confers, whether or not it is moral to use human embryos or other human reproductive tissues for stem-cell research, and whether or not cloning is morally acceptable.

Mainstream religions vary greatly in their policies toward homosexuality. Some view the form of sexuality as a sin, but emphasize that condemnation applies to the sexual act only, and not to the people concerned. Other groups believe homosexuals can be converted to heterosexuality through prayer and religious intervention. Followers of some religions may believe that only heterosexual marriages should be legal, although some Christian churches now readily accept gay ministers. Attempts to pass a constitutional amendment proclaiming marriage as the union

The Religious Coalition for Reproductive Choice

Just when we think we have it straight—liberals, Democrats, and nonreligious people are on one side of the argument over abortion, and conservatives, Republicans, and churchgoers are on the opposite side—a story like the following appears in the media.

The Religious Coalition for Reproductive Choice is a group whose members are religious, but are also pro-choice on matters of reproduction, such as abortion and birth control. "We are not pro-choice in spite of our faith, we are pro-choice because our faith instructs us," said seminarian Kelli Clement in an article that appeared in the March 4, 2008, issue of the *Minnesota Monitor*. Clement, a member of the Unitarian Universalist Church, had an abortion when she was in her twenties and addicted to alcohol, but said, "I have never regretted my choice to terminate that pregnancy. It was the most loving thing I could do."

Clement said that religious individuals who take a more "nuanced" view might come to see the abortion issue as separate from their religious beliefs, as she does. "We need to become comfortable with . . . a broader, more liberal view of God."

The cloning of Dolly, the sheep, in 1997, led to a hue and cry over the possibility of human cloning, which remains illegal in the United States. People have expressed religious and ethical qualms about cloning as well as stem-cell research, though the latter is much more widely supported by mainstream Americans.

between one man and one woman have failed in the United States, but in 1996, the U.S. Congress passed the Defense of Marriage Act. The act denies federal recognition of same-sex marriages and gives each state the right to refuse to recognize same-sex marriage licenses obtained in other states.

The act does not prohibit states from allowing same-sex marriages and does not obligate states to recognize same-sex marriages performed in other states, but, increasingly, many do. Many states have passed laws against same-sex marriage, most recently in California, but some states allow civil unions for same-sex couples, which afford some of the same legal rights to gay couples that are available to heterosexual married couples. These rights include naming a same-sex partner as the "spouse" for health insurance coverage and for receiving the pension benefits of the deceased or divorced partner.

In Connecticut, Iowa, Vermont, and Massachusetts, however, marriage between same-sex couples is legal. In New Jersey, though termed civil unions, same-sex couples have the same rights as those granted by marriage. As of 2008, the legality of same-sex marriage bans in many states had been challenged in court, and many of the cases had been or were scheduled to be decided in state supreme courts. The U.S. Supreme Court, however, has not agreed to hear a same-sex marriage case to date.

Opinions about cloning, or the process of asexually creating genetically identical cells, often involve religious views. Research designed to clone human beings is currently against federal law in the United States. Many crops and even animals used for food have been successfully cloned. There is no federal law against cloning in the United States, but several attempts have been made to pass a Human Cloning Prohibition Act, the last failing in 2007. Several states, however, have laws against human cloning.

Congress has passed laws against federal funding for any research that involves human embryos, which includes stem-cell research. (Stem cells, which are capable of differentiating into a variety of tissues, such as muscles, nerves, skin, and so on, are readily available in embryonic cells.) President Obama, however, reversed those laws in March 2009.

In the United States, some religious people may object to scientific research that involves cloning or the use of embryonic tissue. In a 2002 survey conducted by the Pew Forum on Religion and

Public Life, more than one in four respondents, or 77 percent, were against human cloning. Among survey respondents there was less agreement on the subject of stem-cell research, with 47 to 39 percent saying the research was more important than the potential destruction of human embryos and should be pursued.

Where respondents defined themselves as religious, the Pew survey revealed that objection to cloning and stem-cell research was more widespread. Fifty-eight percent of respondents identified as white evangelical Protestants objected to stem-cell research, and more than seven in ten of all religious groups objected to human cloning. In general, the Pew survey determined that people with high religious commitment were more likely than those with low religious commitment to object to cloning and stem-cell research.

Since the founding of the American republic, religious citizens have been an influential force in society, encouraging moral behavior and advocating for laws to regulate humanity's more primitive instincts. Religion's influence on society in the future, however, faces challenges that have never before been experienced, as the rapid advancement of science and technology threatens ages-old concepts of right and wrong, faith and disbelief, and tolerance and prejudice.

Additional challenges for religion will also arise as the world's increasingly global community interacts. Because religious values in some cultures may tend to be nonnegotiable, religious warfare around the world has become commonplace—in Israel and Palestine; Iraq and Iran; Afghanistan, Pakistan, and India; Rwanda, the Ivory Coast, and Chad; Bosnia-Herzegovina, Kosovo-Albania, Serbia, Croatia, and Uzbekistan; Spain, Cyprus, and Holland; Brazil, Peru, and Haiti—a seemingly endless list of conflicts involving religion.

Although religion and politics are subjects that most Americans avoid in polite company, people in many parts of the world think differently. Understanding those differences is vital to U.S. international relations in the future, and possibly to U.S. security.

6 Foreign Affairs

CLEARLY, THE SEPARATION OF CHURCH AND STATE has long been debated within the United States. The question when dealing with foreign governments, however, has not been whether or not religion should enter into the dialogue (in the past it seldom has), but rather: Does ignorance of religions other than Christianity hamper America's relationships with foreign countries?

The question arises from the two schools of thought that the U.S. government uses in dealing with other nations. The idealistic school of thought concerning America's foreign policy contends that all forms of interaction between countries—economic, as in trade; militaristic, as in police actions and military bases; diplomatic, as in official visits and treaties; and social, as in tourism and extended visits—must at some point take place between people. And if people are concerned about the welfare of others, an attitude that is allegedly established by religious teachings, this will be reflected in dealings with other nations.

This manner of looking at foreign relations derives from the traditional belief of Americans that their country is exceptional —a beacon of freedom and enlightenment for less well-developed nations. This viewpoint encourages Americans to become missionaries—both in the religious sense, in bringing Christianity to people in other nations, and in the political sense, in encouraging the spread of democracy worldwide.

A second school of thought among foreign policy analysts

Some in America are religious about democracy. Above, a U.S. marine carries the American flag across the sands near the border between Saudi Arabia and Kuwait during Operation Desert Storm in 1991.

—realism—cautions against believing that nations will behave like people. Dean Acheson, who served as President Harry S. Truman's secretary of state, subscribed to this school of thought. He wrote in 1964, "A good deal of trouble comes from the anthropomorphic urge to regard nations as individuals and apply to our own national conduct, for instance, the Golden Rule—even though in practice individuals rarely adopt it. The fact is that nations are not individuals; the cause and effect of their actions are wholly different." Nations, this premise holds, will always behave to secure their own interests, with no regard for the morality of their actions.

George Kennan, another foreign policy realist who served as ambassador to the Soviet Union (now Russia) under Truman and as ambassador to Yugoslavia (now Bosnia-Herzegovina, Croatia, Macedonia, Montenegro, Serbia, Slovenia, and Kosovo) under President John F. Kennedy, wrote in the 1980s, "The interests of a national society for which a government has to concern itself are basically those of its military security, the integrity of its political life, and the well-being of its people. These needs have no moral quality. . . . They are the unavoidable necessities of a national existence and therefore not subject to classification as either 'good' or 'bad'."

Kennan, who died in 2005 at the age of 101, was largely responsible for the United States' foreign policy of containment implemented during Truman's administration, under which the American government worked to thwart what was perceived as the Soviet Union's goals of expanding communism.

Over time, the United States' foreign policy has been a mixture of the two schools of thought, sometimes concerned with spreading democracy and with moral principles such as human rights, and other times forced to be realistic, as when siding with dictators and human-rights abusers to achieve larger goals, such as forming alliances to prevent nuclear proliferation or to protect weaker nations from military aggressors.

What many Americans consider moral, however, or the right course to pursue, can be seen as an arrogant and unwanted intervention by the country being helped and by the rest of the world. For example, when U.S. President George H. W. Bush attacked Iraqi dictator Saddam Hussein's troops in Kuwait during the Persian Gulf War in 1991, he expected one result to be that the Iraqi people would drive Hussein from power—a right and moral outcome, in Bush's opinion. This did not happen, so the United States instituted "temporary" economic sanctions against Iraq that lasted for more than ten years. The sanctions did not apply to medicine or food, but the Iraqi economy suffered, the Iraqi people were deprived, and many countries criticized this action.

Furthermore, Hussein took advantage of international sympathy and worked a corrupt oil-for-food scheme that did not benefit the Iraqi people. The oil-for-food program, established by the United Nations in 1995 and ended in late 2003, was intended to allow Iraq to sell oil on the world market in exchange for food, medicine, and other humanitarian needs for ordinary Iraqi citizens without allowing Iraq to rebuild its military. The program was allegedly abused when funds were unlawfully diverted to the Iraqi government and certain U.N. officials. Still, no matter what dictates foreign policy—idealism or realism—a nonviolent solution, such as the use of diplomacy, cannot be found for some conflicts. If two sides of an international dispute have vastly different views of what the outcome should be and are pursuing different goals or different views of what the world should become, it may be impossible to find a solution in which both sides get something they want.

For example, during World War II, the Axis Powers (Germany, Japan, Italy, Hungary, Romania, and Bulgaria) and the Allies (the United States, England, France, Soviet Union, Belgium, Australia, and several other countries) were fighting for completely different goals and visions of the future. Similarly, today fundamentalist followers of Islam are so obsessed with pursuing a *jihad*—a holy war against heretics and infidels (unbelievers)—that their demands cannot be met by the rest of the world. For instance, Islamic terrorist groups, such as Al Qaeda, who frequently attack civilians around the world, have declared that the only concession they want from infidels is for them to die.

Americans have been the victims of the Islamic jihad on several occasions, as when a Marine barracks in Beirut was bombed on October 23, 1983, during the Lebanese civil war, killing 241 American soldiers. The first Islamic attack to occur on American soil was in 1993, when members of the Al Qaeda terrorist group allegedly planted a bomb in the underground parking garage of the World Trade Center in New York City, killing six people and injuring scores more. The second attack on an American target occurred when Al Qaeda terrorists hijacked four commercial airlines, flew two into the World Trade Center towers in New York City, and sent a third into the Pentagon building in Washington, D.C., on September 11, 2001, killing about 3,000 people. Passengers on the fourth plane, which was believed to be headed for the U.S. Capitol, rose up against the hijackers, and the plane crashed into a field in Pennsylvania, killing everyone aboard. After these attacks, American troops invaded Afghanistan.

The expressed purpose of the invasion of Afghanistan was to find and capture Osama Bin Laden, a wealthy Al Qaeda leader who had allegedly planned the 9/11 attacks from his base in Afghanistan, and to destroy Al Qaeda training camps located there. Another objective was to topple the Taliban, a repressive, fanatical Islamic group that supported Al Qaeda and had ruled Afghanistan since 1996. The primary goal may have also been retaliatory, but secondary goals were to free the people of Afghanistan from a repressive government and help them create a democracy.

Again, however, results were often seen in the eyes of the rest of the world as an intrusion that cost the lives of many Afghan citizens and soldiers—Afghan, American, and other nationalities—and did little to permanently eliminate the Taliban and Al Qaeda or to establish a better way of life for Afghans.

When American troops invaded Iraq in 2003, as part of a mission dubbed Operation Iraqi Freedom, motives were again retaliatory, but also idealistic. The United States sought help from other nations, and as of August 23, 2006, at least twenty-one countries (some sources say thirty countries) had sent troops to join those of the United States in Iraq. These combined forces were called coalition forces and included Albania, Armenia, Australia, Azerbaijan, Bosnia-Herzegovina, Bulgaria, Czech Republic, Denmark, El Salvador, Estonia, Georgia, Hungary, Kazakhstan, Latvia, Lithuania, Macedonia, Moldova, Mongolia, Poland, Romania, South Korea, and the United Kingdom. As of fall 2008, American forces remained in Iraq, but most coalition forces had withdrawn.

The Bush administration's stated goals in dispatching American military forces were to search for weapons of mass destruction that the Iraqi regime may have manufactured and stockpiled, and to free the Iraqi people from Saddam Hussein's repressive rule. Furthermore, President George W. Bush said, his administration hoped through military action to control terrorism arising from Iraq, and to help the Iraqis establish a democratic form of government. People around the world soon realized, however, that while America's goals may have seemed reasonable to President Bush, the results fell far short of his stated goals. It was quickly apparent that there were no weapons of mass destruction stockpiled in Iraq, it was never conclusively determined that Al Qaeda maintained terrorist training camps there, and establishing a democratic form of government proved difficult.

As of March 2009, American military casualties were about 4,250 U.S. confirmed dead and more than 30,000 wounded. (The number of American military casualties in Iraq and Afghanistan rose to over 4,800 in March 2009, when soldiers killed in Afghanistan were added to the count.) Non-U.S. coalition forces reportedly lost about 500 soldiers in Iraq.

Civilian casualties in Iraq and Afghanistan are difficult to estimate, since different sources provide different figures. In early 2008, anywhere from 780,000 to more than one million Iraqi deaths were attributed to the war, depending upon the reporting sources.

According to Stephen Prothero, chair of the Department of Religion at Boston University, and author of *Religious Literacy: What Every American Needs to Know About Religion—And Doesn't*, one major reason for the failure of the Bush administration to accomplish goals in Iraq was ignorance of the country's religion. Government officials may have understood the politics, economy, and ethnicity of Iraq, Prothero told the audience at the Pew Forum Faith Angle Conference in Key West, Florida, in December 2007, "But I don't think we understood it as a religious place, where religious reasons mattered, where people were, perhaps in many cases, primarily motivated by religion."

History has reinforced the lesson that failing to recognize that religion influences foreign relations has been costly to the United States. In the early 1960s, American foreign policy, under President John F. Kennedy and later under Presidents Lyndon B. Johnson and Richard M. Nixon, consisted largely of attempts to contain the advancement of communism around the world. This was the time of the Cold War, when the Communist threat dominated U.S. foreign relations. In line with the containment policy, in 1965 the United States sent military troops into Vietnam to prevent the collapse of the South Vietnamese government, which was under siege from Communist troops in North Vietnam. The war in Vietnam was fought largely over political ideology and nationalism, but it also had a religious component. Surveys taken in the 1960s showed that approximately 70 percent of the Vietnamese population followed Buddhism. The French who had occupied Vietnam until 1954 were largely Catholic and under their rule, 10 percent of the citizens of South Vietnam had converted to Catholicism. The French were aware of the threat that Buddhism posed to their authority, and passed laws to limit its growth while they were in power.

On May 8, 1963, Buddhist worshippers assembled in Hue, South Vietnam, to celebrate the 2,527th birthday of the Buddha. The president of South Vietnam, Ngo Dinh Diem, was Catholic and had appointed many Catholics to positions in his government. Diem's police attempted to disperse the Buddhist celebrants by firing into the crowd, and a woman and eight children were killed as they tried to flee. The Buddhists were furious and held many public demonstrations to protest, but Diem refused to repeal any of the anti-Buddhist laws that the French had passed.

Finally, in June 1963, Thich Quang Due (sometimes spelled "Duc"), a sixty-six-year-old Buddhist monk, sat down in the middle of a busy Saigon road and voluntarily allowed Buddhist monks and nuns to douse him with gasoline and then set him on fire in protest. Witnesses said the monk did not make a sound or move a muscle while the fire raged. While Thich Quang Due was burning to death, the monks and nuns distributed flyers that called for the government to show "charity and compassion" to all religions. Diem's response to the suicide was to arrest thousands of Buddhist monks, a number of whom were never heard from again.

By August 1963 five more Buddhist monks had set fire to themselves. One member of the South Vietnamese government responded to the suicides by telling a newspaper reporter: "Let them burn, and we shall clap our hands." Another offered to supply Buddhists who wanted to commit suicide with the necessary gasoline. Diem, whose government the United States was backing, declared martial law to control the riots and restore order. International news photographers captured the suicides, and to much of the world the United States appeared to be backing the wrong side.

The United States began withdrawing troops from Vietnam in 1973. In April 1975, as the first tanks from North Vietnam smashed through the gates of the presidential palace in Saigon, the last U.S. helicopter lifted off from the roof of the American Embassy, marking the end of the American presence in Vietnam. A total of 58,000 American troops died in Vietnam and more than 300,000 were wounded. After the war, the Vietnamese government in Hanoi released the figures for civilian dead: 2 million in North Vietnam and 2 million in South Vietnam. Based on a total Vietnamese population of approximately 38 million at the time, the civilian death toll equaled approximately 12 to 13 percent of the entire population of Vietnam. Since the war ended, North and South Vietnam, which are presently united as one country, have remained under Communist rule.

When President Jimmy Carter took office in 1977, he inherited from previous administrations a friendly relationship with Mohammad Reza Pahlavi, the shah of Iran. The United States had maintained a working relationship with the shah since 1953, the year the U.S. Central Intelligence Agency (CIA) engineered a coup that ousted an elected but anti-Western Iranian prime minister and installed the shah. Once in control, the shah proved to be a ruthless dictator whose secret police were widely feared for their expertise in torture.

A little noticed event in Iran in the 1960s was the shah's ouster of an obscure Iranian Shi'ite cleric, Ayatollah Ruhollah Khomeini, who protested the shah's regime. Khomeini fled to France, but continued to communicate with the Iranian people via telephone and smuggled cassette tapes. While Khomeini secretly amassed loyal followers in Iran, the shah killed the cleric's son, declared martial law, and ordered his troops to shoot at a crowd of unarmed demonstrators, killing 900.

The U.S. government was alarmed at the turmoil in Iran, but President Carter's administration continued to support the shah,

In America, Christianity is the dominant religion, but that is not the case in much of the world. In 2006, Muslim protesters held placards as they burned portraits of Pope Benedict XVI in response to his controversial remarks about Islam and jihad.

even when he refused to adopt reforms that might restore calm. The Iranian people constantly revolted against the shah, through violent public demonstrations and strikes, and when he finally left the country in 1979, Khomeini returned to seize power. He declared a new Islamic Republic, where all laws governing the country were based on the Islamic holy book, the Koran. Khomeini whipped his followers into an anti-American frenzy that some sources believe has led to an ongoing hatred in Iran of all things American.

After the shah was deposed, on November 4, 1979, Iranian student militants stormed the U.S. embassy in Tehran and captured sixty-six U.S. diplomats and other employees stationed there. President Carter made an ill-advised attempt to rescue the hostages via helicopter, but the helicopter crashed before reaching its destination and the rescue mission failed. The hostages were released a few at a time through 1979 and 1980, and all fifty-two remaining captives were freed on January 20, 1981. The hostage crisis lasted a total of 444 days.

Madeleine Albright, former member of the National Security Council, U.S. ambassador to the United Nations, and secretary of state under President Bill Clinton, writes of that time in *The Mighty and the Almighty*: "We were caught off guard by the revolution in Iran for the simple reason that we had never seen anything like it. As a political force, Islam was thought to be waning, not rising. Everyone in the region was presumed to be preoccupied with the practical problems of economics and modernization. A revolution in Iran based on a religious backlash against America and the West? Other than a few fanatics, who would support such a thing?" The situation in Iran brought home to the U.S. government in no uncertain terms that in foreign affairs religion counts.

One reason the revolution in Iran was so shocking to American policymakers was that, up to that time, they had no preparation in terms of learning about religion in other parts of the world and no source of advice on the topic within the government. Albright writes: "When I was secretary of state, I had an entire bureau of economic experts I could turn to, and a cadre of experts on non-proliferation and arms control whose mastery of technical jargon earned them a nickname, 'the priesthood'." Albright had no one within the government to whom she could turn for advice and instruction on combining religious principles with diplomacy.

"Given the nature of today's world, knowledge of this type is essential," she adds.

In 1994, as it was becoming increasingly clear that religion matters in foreign relations, the Center for Strategic and International Studies published *Religion, the Missing Dimension of Statecraft.* About the same time the book was published, its coauthor, Douglas Johnston, a former naval officer and senior official in the U.S. Department of Defense, founded the International Center for Religion and Diplomacy (ICRD) to study faith-based diplomacy and play a mediating role in some of the world's religious conflicts, such as those in Pakistan, Iran, and the Sudan. A second book, *Faith-Based Diplomacy: Trumping Realpolitik* continues Johnston's premise that religion should be an integral part of U.S. foreign policy.

Why is religion important to international relations? In a speech delivered to a U.S. Department of State Open Forum in December 2006, Johnston explained that in nearly every current global conflict there is a religious component, as in Iraq, Afghanistan, Lebanon, Nigeria, Sri Lanka, Kashmir, Sudan, Indonesia, Chechnya, Kosovo, and other areas around the globe: "Whether religion is a root cause of the conflict as it probably comes closest to being in the Middle East (where there are competing religious claims for the same piece of territory), or merely a badge of identity and mobilizing vehicle for nationalist or ethnic passions (as has typically been the case in the Balkans), it is nevertheless central to much of the strife that is taking place."

The United States has had difficulty dealing effectively with religious conflicts, Johnston claims, because our diplomats approach global strife from two positions:

1. Rational decision-making, which views religion as irrational and therefore excludes it from the process.
2. Separation of church and state, which is ingrained in American political thought, and therefore carries over into international relations.

Separating religion from government is a foreign concept to those who follow the Islamic faith, Johnston states. "We say 'secular;' they hear 'Godless,' when what was intended was 'freedom to worship as you please.' They hear 'Godless' in large part because of the cultural image we project."

At the very least, American diplomats hoping to communicate with Muslims in foreign countries should be aware that "Sunni" refers to a member of the larger of the two primary denominations of Islam. Shi'ite Muslims comprise 10 to 15 percent of all Muslims. They split from the Sunni majority over the issue of who should be Mohammed's successor.

The ICRD trains religious scholars on all sides of a conflict who then discuss possible solutions. In the Sudan, for example, in 2000, the ICRD brought together thirty scholars—Sudanese Muslims and Christian leaders-—to participate in a four-day conference to discuss

Anti-United States fervor runs high in Iran. A female Iranian in a chador passes by a painting of a revolver in front of the former U.S. embassy in Tehran.

Just as each country varies in terms of which religion is most dominant among its population, countries also vary widely in the degree of separation between their governments and religion, and the degree to which their governments grant religious freedom. In fact, the promotion of religious freedom in countries around the world has become a core objective of the United States' foreign policy and an important mission of the U.S. Department of State.

Most European countries have constitutions that grant religious freedom, and most protect this freedom. Some designate a state religion, which means that they may also support the state religion through public monies.

The United Kingdom (UK), which includes England, Wales, Scotland, and Northern Ireland, protects freedom of religion constitutionally and prohibits discrimination based on religion through laws that include the Human Rights Act; Employment Equality Regulations; the Anti-Terrorism, Crime, and Security Act; and the Racial and Religious Hatred Act. The UK has two established, or state, churches: the Church of England (Anglican) and the Church of Scotland (Presbyterian). The government has emphasized that the establishment of state churches is deeply ingrained in the nation's history, but does not preclude citizens from joining other churches or practicing the religions of their choice.

France practices a more complete separation of church and state than the UK. A 1905 law on the separation of church and state prohibits discrimination on the basis of religion. The French Constitution of the Fifth Republic, adopted in 1958, declares the country to be "an indivisible, secular, democratic, and social Republic."

French citizens have a variety of constitutional rights, including the presumption of innocence, the guarantee of property ownership against arbitrary seizure, accountability of government agents to the citizens, freedom of speech, freedom of opinion, and freedom of religion. France does not designate or support a state religion, but those who practice the Jewish, Catholic, Lutheran, and Reformed

A young Muslim girl wears two French flags and a headband reading *Fraternité* (Brotherhood) on her headscarf as part of a protest by three thousand Sikhs against the proposed French ban on wearing conspicuous religious symbols in schools. The ban was passed.

religions may designate a portion of their income tax payments to go to their church. Private schools, including religious schools, are subsidized by the government. In 2004 the French government passed a law that banned wearing conspicuous religious symbols in public schools, which included the headscarves female Muslims typically wear, yarmulkes worn by Jews, and large crosses. Furthermore, a government commission on sects established in 1996 designated the Jehovah's Witnesses a criminal sect because of their prohibition on blood transfusions.

While Article 4 of Germany's Basic Law for the Federal Republic guarantees citizens freedom of faith, creed, conscience, and the practice of religion, in recent years the country has come under attack for its treatment of certain religious minorities. Three faiths —Lutheran, Catholic, and Jewish—enjoy special corporate status under the law, which allows them specific tax advantages. Church schools receive government subsidies and public schools provide religious instruction in the three favored faiths. Minority religions may be tax-exempt, but the German government has been accused of discriminating against some minority religions. For example, Scientologists, who follow the Scientology religion, developed by the late L. Ron Hubbard, a former science-fiction writer, may not join a major political party in Germany. A ban had been sought against the performances of Scientologist musicians and actors in Germany, but it didn't take effect. Films starring Tom Cruise and John Travolta, American Scientologist actors, were boycotted by a Youth Union group in Germany, but nevertheless did very well.

In another example of discrimination against a minority religion, members of the Unification Church, founded by the Reverend Sun Myung Moon, have been banned from entering Germany as part of the nation's anticult campaign. (Bans against members of the Unification Church are also in place in Austria, Belgium, France, Luxembourg, Portugal, and Spain for the same reason the religion is banned in Germany—as part of government-ordered anticult campaigns.) The church has also been denied tax-exempt status in Germany, the stated reason being that it is a "danger to the public good." Unification Church beliefs are based on Moon's book, *Divine Principle*, and include a belief in a universal God; in the creation of a Kingdom of Heaven on Earth; and the possibility of salvation for all people, good and evil, as well as living and dead. Unification Church members are also taught that Jesus did not come to Earth for the express purpose of dying, and that the second coming of Christ was a man born in Korea in the early twentieth century—Sun Myung Moon, the man who founded the Unification Church.

Like the constitutions of most European countries, Italy's constitution provides for freedom of religion and the government generally protects this freedom in practice. The Roman Catholic Church's long association with the government has resulted in some concessions to that religion, but as of 1984, the nation's

The Reverend Sun Myung Moon has had a huge following. Though his church is banned in Germany, it has experienced bias throughout much of the world, because it is considered by many to be a cult rather than a religious organization. Its many members disagree. Here, the Reverend Moon presides over a mass wedding of 22,000 couples in Madison Square Garden in New York.

constitution has declared that the government and the Roman Catholic Church are independent and sovereign. In 1984 an agreement was signed between the government and the Vatican, stating that Catholicism would no longer be Italy's state religion and that Rome would no longer retain the "sacred character of eternal city" (Vatican City, the official government ruled by the Pope, is located within the city of Rome). Members of the Roman Catholic Church, Assembly of God Church, and the Adventist Church may make arrangements to have a portion of their taxes donated to their respective churches.

Spain's constitution also grants religious freedom to citizens. The government subsidizes the Catholic Church, but Jewish and Protestant leaders in Spain have declined government help.

This table illustrates how governments in other countries relate to religion:

Separation of Church and State as Practiced Around the World

Country	Constitution Grants Religious Freedom	State-Designated Religion	Tax Subsidies	Mandatory Religious Instruction in Public Schools
Norway	Yes	Yes—Evangelical-Lutheran	Yes	Yes
Greece	Yes, with some stipulations	Yes—Eastern Orthodox	Yes	Yes, for Orthodox students only
Hungary	Yes	No	Yes—largely to four major religions	No
Turkey	Yes, with some restrictions	No, but most citizens are Muslim	Yes	Yes
Russia	Yes, with legal restrictions on many denominations other than Russian Orthodox	No, but Russian Orthodox is the dominant religion	Yes, for Russian Orthodox Church	Yes, for Russian Orthodox students
India	Yes	No, but the dominant religion is Hindu and there are clashes between Hindus and Muslims and Hindus and Christians	Yes, legally mandated benefits are assigned to certain groups	No
China	No—religious repression existed until the 1980s; religious revival continues to the present	No—Buddhism and Daoism dominate and the government recognizes and monitors five religions through "patriotic associations"	No—religious activity is highly regulated and restricted	No
Japan	Yes	No—Buddhism and Shinto dominant, cults regulated and restricted—called "modern day mental illness"	No, but are tax exempt if registered as "religious corporation"	No
Iran	No—the government is a theocracy	Yes—Islam—other religions severely restricted	Yes	Yes

During Madeleine Albright's tenure as secretary of state, in 1998, Congress passed the International Religious Freedom Act, to promote religious freedom as a goal of U.S. international relations policy. The act established within the U.S. Department of State:

- An ambassador at large for religious freedom
- An Office of International Religious Freedom within the U.S. Department of State
- A bipartisan commission on international religious freedom
- Within the National Security Council a special advisor on international religious freedom

The U.S. Department of State's Office of International Religious Freedom promotes freedom of religion throughout the world as an inalienable human right. The office seeks to:

- Promote freedom of religion and conscience within every nation as a basic human right and as a measure of stability of a nation's government
- Advise and assist new democracies in establishing and nurturing freedom of religion and conscience
- Assist religious and human rights nongovernmental organizations in promoting freedom of religion
- Identify and denounce governments that persecute individuals based on their religious beliefs

Under the auspices of the Freedom of Religion Act, the U.S. Department of State prepares an annual International Religious Freedom Report, using information provided by American embassies around the world and a variety of other sources. The report names those countries where religious freedom is denied, with the intention of impeding the progress of religious persecution in those countries. The process used to prepare the report—investigating, documenting, and protesting abuses—has helped to prevent or tone down some religious persecution that would otherwise occur.

As the reports are compiled, the U.S. Department of State also prepares a list of "Countries of Particular Concern" under the International Religious Freedom Act. Those countries listed are then subject to a U.S. actions that usually include economic sanctions.

The Department of State uses the following list of possible abuses to determine whether a country should be listed as one of particular concern. The countries on this list in 2006 included Burma (known in the United States as Myanmar), China, Eritrea, Iran, North Korea, Saudi Arabia, and Sudan:

- Totalitarian and authoritarian regimes may attempt to control religious thought and action. Such regimes regard some or all religions as enemies of the state and persecute them accordingly.
- Governments may be hostile to minority or non-state-approved religions, intimidating or harassing them.
- The state may simply fail to address either societal discrimination or societal abuses against religious groups. Legislation may discourage such abuse, but officials fail to prevent it.
- Governments pass discriminatory laws against certain minority or non-state-sanctioned religions.
- Governments discriminate against certain religions by designating them as dangerous cults or sects.

In addition to the countries on its list, the United Nations (UN) is also concerned with the status of religious freedom around the world. In the UN's Universal Declaration of Human Rights of 1948, citizens of every nation were proclaimed to possess certain human rights, including the right to freedom of religion.

Similarly, the International Covenant on Civil and Political Rights, initiated by the UN's Office of the High Commissioner for Human Rights (OHCHR) in 1966, proclaimed the right of all people to "self-determination," which included the right to "freely determine their political status and freely pursue their economic, social, and cultural development."

The UN's Human Rights Commission appointed an unpaid special rapporteur, who visits various countries and reports on their successes or failures in respecting the population's human rights. Both the declaration and the covenant set forth human rights similar to those in the American Bill of Rights, but the UN has had little authority to enforce these rights or to punish those nations that consistently ignore them.

The United States and the United Nations are concerned about religious freedom around the world because religious freedom is closely associated with all civil liberties. If freedom of speech is restricted in a country, generally religious speech is also restricted. If freedom to assemble is not allowed, it follows that assembling for worship is not allowed. Where men are viewed as religious heads of households, women's rights are generally severely restricted. And if a country has little tolerance for the freedom not to worship, failure to attend a state-sanctioned church (or any church) can result in severe penalties in countries where religious freedom is absent, such as harassment, torture, and even death. It is crucial, therefore, that governments respect all human rights, so that each individual freedom is equally protected.

Furthermore, religious liberty is strongly associated with political, social, and ethnic identity, which makes it integral to one's deepest belief systems. For this reason, it is understandable that citizens want their government to reflect those morals and principles that form the core of their personal belief. The question remains, however, when belief systems vary with individuals, if the government becomes involved in furthering or hindering any one religion or specific religions, who will choose the religion(s) to be favored? And will it become easy for governments, made up of individuals, to persecute those associated with religions that are not so favored?

In any discussion of the status of freedom of religion around the world, it is also important to remember that nonbelievers, in a country under a government that respects human rights, have the same rights as believers. Just as Muslims, Catholics, Protestants, Jews, Buddhists, Hindus, and all believers should have the basic human right to worship when, where, and how they please, so, too, must nonbelievers have the right not to worship at all.

In a recent article in *Newsweek*, Lisa Miller proclaims, "What's dangerous about the world today is not belief in God—or secularism or unbelief—but ruthless certainty. If 2008 is the year when we can begin, in private and in public, to concede that we don't know all the answers, then let us say amen."

8 When Religion Rules

PICTURE THIS SCENE FROM IRAN, 2006: SEVERAL friends decide to go shopping at the mall. There are four young women in the group. Three wear makeup and brightly colored skirts, blouses, and headscarves, while the fourth, whose parents are strict, does not wear makeup and has dressed all in black. Three young men who are also in the group wear short-sleeved shirts and have chosen popular hairstyles. As the group approaches the mall entrance, two policemen jump from a police car parked in front of the mall and arrest all but one member of the group for "inappropriate dress." The girl without makeup, her hair completely covered by a black *hijab*, dressed in a black, long-sleeved, floor-length garment called a *chador*, does not argue with the police as the other girls do, and she is not arrested.

Such a scene does not occur in the United States, but it is typical in some Middle Eastern countries where religious leaders are part of government and laws are determined by religious beliefs. In Iran, where such scenes actually take place regularly, the government often cracks down on young people who become lax in following Islamic dictates for dress and public behavior. Countries ruled wholly or in part by religious leaders are called theocracies, and Iran is one such country.

Iranians have lived under strict Islamic law (Shari'a) since Iran's constitution was rewritten after the 1979 revolution, to conform to the Koran. Article 4 of the Iranian constitution says: "All laws

An Iranian policewoman (left) warns a woman about her Western clothing and not entirely covered hair during a crackdown to enforce the Islamic dress code. Women are not allowed outside in Iran unless they are completely covered by a garment called a *chador.*

and regulations including civil, criminal, financial, economic, administrative, cultural, military, political or otherwise, shall be based on Islamic principles. This Article shall apply generally to all the Articles of the Constitution and to other laws and regulations."

After the American-supported shah departed in 1979, Ayatollah Ruhollah Khomeini, a revered *imam* (Muslim religious leader), assumed power as the supreme leader of Iran. As provided in the constitution, the supreme leader is the highest official state authority (Article 113). He is chosen by the Leadership Experts (LE) or leadership *Khobregan,* a division of the *Faqihs* (jurist counsults on religious law). All members of LE must be clergymen and they supervise the supreme leader, who is also a clergyman.

Iran's constitution also provides for the election of a president, whose duties are restricted to the implementation of the constitution.

All other governmental authority falls to the supreme leader. The president is elected by direct vote of the people. The judicial branch of government and representatives of the *Majlis* (Islamic Consultative Assembly), who are also elected, supervise the president.

While the constitution of the Islamic Republic of Iran also calls for three branches of government—legislative, executive, and judicial—the authority of the supreme leader supersedes that of all other branches and offices of government. In fact, if the supreme leader violates the constitution using Islamic rules for justification, no one is empowered to oppose him.

Once the 1979 constitution was in place, the Ayatollah Ruhollah Khomeini formally assumed his position as supreme leader. Khomeini died on June 4, 1989, at the age of eighty-seven. Tehran Radio announced the death, illustrating the reverence with which faithful Muslim Iranians held the spiritual and political leader: "The lofty spirit of the leader of the Muslims and the leader of the noble ones, His Eminence Imam Khomeini, has reached the highest status, and a heart replete with love and God and his true people, who have endured numerous hardships, has stopped beating."

On the day of the deceased imam's burial, Ayatollah Khomeini's body, wrapped in a white burial shroud, was laid in an open coffin, and carried to Behesht-e-Zahra, the burial site. Members of the crowd along the route, hysterical with grief, grabbed at the body, hoping to tear away a piece of the shroud to keep as a memento. The men holding the litter were jostled, the burial box tipped, and the Ayatollah's body fell to the ground. Revolutionary Guards escorting the funeral procession beat back the crowd while the ruler's body was replaced in its burial box. A helicopter hovering overhead dropped low enough to snatch the body and carry it away from the grief-stricken mourners. Hours later, the Ayatollah reached his final resting place.

The Khomeini era, which lasted ten years, is known for redefining Iran as a republic ruled by the laws of Islam.

Though vilified in the West, Ayatollah Ruhollah Khomeini was revered by his loyal Muslim followers. Iranian Muslims publicly mourned his death in June 1989.

Today Ayatollah Ali Khamenei is the supreme leader of the Islamic Republic of Iran. In his position as spiritual head of the government, Khamenei has designated prayer leaders in each city and representatives in each major government office that give him eyes and ears everywhere. Furthermore, he selects the members of the Guardian Council, which must approve all legislation passed by the parliament, or Majlis. He closely controls the country's radio and television networks, whose director he appoints. He also appoints the heads of the clerical court and the regular judiciary, who in turn appoint the nation's other judges. He is also head of the seminary system (*rais-e howzeh*).

In addition, Khamenei controls the key instruments of national security: the Islamic Revolutionary Guard Corps (IRGC), the politically active Basij paramilitary, and the KGB-like Ministry of Intelligence and Security (charged with security operations both at home and abroad). Nuclear negotiations with the West are conducted by Khamenei's representative with little or no input from the Ministry of Foreign Affairs.

Iran's president, Mahmoud Ahmadinejad, took office in 2005, after winning the popular vote. Ahmadinejad, the son of a blacksmith, worked in the internal security office of the IRGC in the 1980s, and earned a reputation as a ruthless interrogator and torturer. In 1997 Ahmadinejad returned to Elm-o Sanaat University to teach, but his principal activity was to organize Ansar-e Hezbollah, a radical gang of violent Islamic vigilantes. When he was elected president in the 2005 election, Ahmadinejad was the ultraconservative Islamic mayor of Tehran.

From an economic standpoint, oil and natural gas earn approximately $1,300 (U.S. dollars) a year for each Iranian. Iran's central bank prints currency, which has pushed inflation up to about 25 percent per year, and unemployment remains at 11 percent. Rural Iranians support the Islamists, because they have been promised government support. Modernists look to the West for inspiration, and many have left Iran to live in other countries where freedom of religion and freedom from Islamic repression exist. In a country where Islam regulates every facet of existence, many cannot imagine their lives outside of Muslim traditionalism. Yet, as the twenty-first century progresses, fewer than three-fourths of Iranian women can read, and the country has one phone line for every five people. Islamic Iran promises protection to its subjects against a threatening outside world, however, and apparently hopes to force other countries to submit to Islamic standards—if only through the threat of nuclear proliferation.

Under President Ahmadinejad, most leaders of the free world believe that the Islamic Republic of Iran will institute increasingly radical policies that will include more human rights abuses, continuing sponsorship of terrorism, and a persistent drive to obtain nuclear weapons.

In today's Iran, under the written word of the Koran, five themes are reinforced by law:

1. The call to worship
2. The need for justice
3. The worthlessness of paganism
4. The inevitability of the Day of Judgment and the punishments for evildoers
5. The reward of paradise for the faithful

Under these mandates, Islamic law calls for the government's enforcement of public morality. Iranian moral offenses, for which the police can arrest violators, include:

a. Terrorizing others by quarreling and feuding in public
b. Women failing to cover up in a suitable way
    i. Legs must not be exposed
    ii. Hats must not be substituted for scarves, which cover the hair
    iii. High-heeled shoes and sandals are not acceptable
    iv. Designer handbags are forbidden
    v. Bejeweled sunglasses are prohibited
c. Women wearing makeup
d. Either sex wearing decadent Western clothing
e. Viewing decadent films
f. Drinking alcohol or taking drugs
g. General thuggish behavior
h. Displaying signs and insignia of deviant groups

Other offenses that can lead to arrest include unmarried couples walking hand-in-hand or sitting together on park benches, a man holding a woman's waist while walking in a shopping complex, sitting on a bench with the woman leaning on the man's shoulder, sitting on a bench in the dark in a park or by a lake, and females being in places that serve alcohol. Police may seize young men with improper hair lengths and forcibly cut their hair.

University students in Iran are warned not to get involved in politics. Those who do may be banned from pursuing chosen degrees, or expelled from school. President Ahmadinejad appointed a cleric to head Tehran University, Iran's most political and prestigious university. The BBC, Britain's national station, reported in 2006 that the first time the new chancellor entered the university, protesting students knocked off his turban—a sign of extreme disrespect for a cleric. Students also displayed signs that read, "This is not a religious seminary—it's a university."

Iranian stores that sell clothing are also subject to government regulations, and in one recent crackdown, store managers were ordered to cut the breasts off of realistically constructed female mannequins. Some shops are sealed, and others are warned not to sell tight, revealing clothing.

These offenses are punishable by jail terms, fines, and caning, depending upon the seriousness of the offense and the behavior of the offender at the time of arrest. Other, more serious morality offenses, such as homosexuality and women who commit adultery (men are seldom punished as adulterers, and can take more than one wife), can be punished by torture and death.

Similarly, in Saudi Arabia, Islamic law controls life for residents. Women—both citizens and visitors—are expected to wear appropriate dress, which means arms, legs, and hair are covered. Muslim Saudi women generally wear the traditional *abaya*, which is a shapeless black, gray, dark blue, or white floor-length garment that covers the entire body, including the arms. Muslim women also wear a scarf that completely covers their hair, and they may also wear a veil to cover their faces. Failure to dress appropriately can result in arrest for Saudi women.

Saudi Arabia's version of Muslim law forbids women to drive

or drink alcohol, and also forbids any citizen to practice Western vices. Cigarettes are allowed, but no public movie theaters, public bowling alleys, bars or nightclubs, and no churches—mosques are the only worship centers that receive government approval. All restaurants have two sections—a single males section and a family section. Women dining as a group with female friends must sit in the family section or risk arrest for prostitution.

As in Iran, Islamic law mandates prayer five times a day for Muslims in Saudi Arabia. In most Middle Eastern countries where Islam is dominant, businesses allow prayer breaks for the faithful, but do not close. In Saudi Arabia, however, stores and restaurants close during prayer times. If shoppers or diners happen to be inside a business when prayer time is called, they are locked in, but can continue to eat or shop. Lights are dimmed, however, so after-dark diners sometimes carry candles if the meal will extend through the mid-evening prayer call.

Afghanistan under Taliban rule was perhaps the strictest of those countries where Islamic law presides. Before the United States and Great Britain invaded Afghanistan in October 2001, the radical Islamic movement called the Taliban controlled approximately 95 percent of the country, including the capital of Kabul, and most of the largest urban areas. (The invasion was in retaliation for the September 11, 2001, attacks on the World Trade Center and the Pentagon, which were allegedly planned by Osama bin Laden, an Al Qaeda leader living in Afghanistan with the Taliban's blessing.)

The pre-invasion Afghanistan government was a brutal, repressive theocracy. A Taliban edict in 1997 renamed the country the Islamic Emirate of Afghanistan, with Taliban leader Mullah (a title of respect for a Muslim cleric) Omar as Head of State and Commander of the Faithful. There was a six-member ruling council in Kabul, but ultimate authority for Taliban rule rested in Mullah Omar, head of the inner Shura (council), located in the southern city of Kandahar. There was no countrywide recognized constitution, rule of law, or independent judiciary, and the Taliban was the country's primary military force and law-enforcement body. In 2000 the country was the largest opium producer in the world.

As is true of most Islamic theocracies, women in Afghanistan were especially oppressed. In fact, under the Taliban, Afghan women suffered a complete loss of human rights. After the Taliban assumed power in 1996, women were required to wear the *burqua* in public, a shapeless garment that covered the entire body. Headscarves and veils were also mandatory, of course, and the veils had to cover the entire face—including the eyes. Women were severely beaten or stoned for appearing in public with any part of their bodies showing.

Women were not allowed to work or to appear in public without a male relative. To appear in public with a man who was not a relative was justification for a woman to receive a public lashing. Married women accused of adultery could be stoned to death. Professional women, including professors, doctors, lawyers, teachers, engineers, artists, and writers, who had careers before the Taliban assumed power were forced to leave their jobs to keep house for their husbands. Households where a woman was present were to have the windows painted over, and women were told to wear soft shoes so that men would not hear them when they walked. If a woman had no man for financial support, she was forced to beg in the streets or starve to death.

Women under Taliban rule were not allowed to attend school (girls' schools were converted to religious seminaries for males only), and there were no medical facilities for women. Husbands had complete control over the lives of female relatives—especially wives—and women lived in constant fear for their lives for the slightest infraction.

Requirements for men—wearing the requisite turban, allowing facial hair to grow, and observing all additional Islamic rules—seem tame by comparison to those restrictions imposed on women.

The 2001 United States/United Kingdom invasion of Afghanistan toppled the Taliban, but because of a reduction in the occupying military forces, the Taliban has since regained some control. As of 2008, the country was still a refuge for Al Qaeda, Osama bin Laden had not been captured and his whereabouts were unknown, the country continued to produce large amounts of opium, and the new democratic government was weak in areas outside of Kabul.

When existing theocracies are examined and compared with those countries that practice separation of church and state, most in the West believe that while freedom of religion must be constitutionally defined and legally maintained, governments best serve citizens and best protect their human rights when they neither embrace nor reject religion.

Clyde Wilcox and Carin Larson, authors of *Onward Christian Soldiers? The Religious Right in American Politics*, remind those on both sides of the separation of church and state issue that because the issue has become divided along political lines, "there has been more shouting than discussion, and both sides have ended up adopting more extreme positions in an effort to mobilize voters. Between the shouting voices there is room for a quieter discussion, where both sides might be surprised that they have some common ground."

Toward the end of finding common ground on which to base rational, reasoned discussion of the separation of church and state issue, we can all, once again, say amen.

Notes

Introduction

p. 5, "Faith-based and other . . .": George Bush, "Executive Order: Establishment of White House Office of Faith-Based and Community Initiatives," January 2001, http://www.whitehouse.gov/news/releases/2001/01/20010129-2.html (accessed September 2, 2008).

Chapter 1

p. 13, "Mrs. Hutchinson, you are . . .": Governor Winthrop quoted in Stephen M Feldman, *Please Don't Wish Me a Merry Christmas: A Critical History of the Separation of Church and State* (New York: New York University Press, 1997), 127.

p. 16, "Faith is the only wedding garment . . .": Feldman, 138.

p. 17, "[Between just 1740 and 1743] thousands were converted . . .": Feldman, 137.

p. 18, "United Colonies are, and of right . . .": Thomas Jefferson, *Declaration of Independence*, June 1776. The National Archives, http://www.archives.gov/exhibits/charters/declaration_transcript.html (accessed September 2, 2008).

p. 21, "No State shall make or enforce any law . . .": U.S. Constitution, amend. 14, sec. 1.

p. 22, "The legitimate powers of government . . .": Thomas Jefferson, *Notes onthe State of Virginia*, quoted in Daniel L. Dreisbach, *Thomas Jefferson and the Wall of Separation Between Church and State* (New York: New York University Press, 2002), 49.

p. 22, "Congress shall make no law . . .": U.S. Constitution, amend. 1, sec. 1.

p. 23, "Here is my creed. I believe in one God . . .": Benjamin Franklin to Ezra Stiles, 9 March 1790. Benjamin Franklin on Religion, World Policy Institute, http://www.worldpolicy.org/projects/globalrights/religion/franklin-religion.html (accessed September 2, 2008).

p. 24, "The liberty enjoyed by the People . . .": George Washington to the Philadelphia Quakers, *Air and Space Power Journal*, July/August 1976, http://www.airpower.maxwell.af.mil/airchronicles/aureview/1976/jul-aug/edavis.html (accessed September 2, 2008).

p. 24, "a necessary spring of popular government": George Washington, "Farewell Address" (speech, September 1796), *The Yale Law School*, http://www.yale.edu/lawweb/avalon/washing.htm (accessed September 2, 2008).

p. 25, "Believing with you . . .": Thomas Jefferson quoted in Dreisbach, 17.

p. 25, "no religious Test. . .": U.S. Constitution, art. 6, cl. 3.

p. 26, "I do solemnly swear . . .": U.S. Constitution, art. 2, sec. 1, cl. 9.

Chapter 2

p. 27, "A Gallup Poll conducted . . .": *Gallup*, "Religion," http://www.gallup.com/poll/1690/Religion.aspx (accessed September 2, 2008).

p. 27, "we may see the Bible cast . . .": Reverend Dwight quoted in Dreisbach, 19.

p. 29, "Governments only concern . . .": Jacob Henry quoted in Jon Meacham, "A New American Holy War," *Newsweek* (December 17, 2007): 33.

p. 30, "We the people . . .": U.S. Constitution, preamble.

p. 30, "We, the people . . . humbly . . .": Morton Borden, "The Christian Amendment," *Civil War History* 25.2 (1979): 156–167.

p. 31, "our entire political . . .": Francis Ellingwood Abbot quoted in Philip Hamburger, *Separation of Church and State* (Cambridge, Massachusetts: Harvard University Press, 2002), 294–295.

p. 32, "My view is that when . . .": Mitt Romney quoted in Meacham, 30.

p. 33, "I think it's a good thing . . .": Mike Huckabee quoted in Ieva M. Augstums, "Huckabee Declines Theology Discussion," *Washington Post*,

December 7, 2007, http://www.washingtonpost.com/wp-dyn/content/article/2007/12/07/AR2007120700942.html (accessed September 2, 2008).

p. 33, "A question posed . . .": *The New York Times*, "The Republicans' First Presidential Candidates Debate transcript, May 3, 2007, http://www.nytimes.com/2007/05/03/us/politics/04transcript.html (accessed September 2, 2008).

p. 35, "the attitude that religion . . .": Stephen L. Carter, *God's Name in Vain: The Wrongs and Rights of Religion in Politics* (New York: Basic Books, 2000), 12, 102.

p. 36, "Let us march . . .": Martin Luther King Jr. quoted in Carter, *God's Name in Vain*, 35.

p. 36, "Religions that most need protection . . .": Stephen L. Carter, *The Culture of Disbelief: How American Law and Politics Trivialize Religious Devotion* (New York: Anchor Books, 1993), 9.

p. 37, "I had nothing to do . . .": James Earl Ray quoted in CNN, "James Earl Ray, Convicted King Assassin, Dies," CNN.com, April 23, 1998, http://www.cnn.com/US/9804/23/ray.obit/ (accessed September 2, 2008).

Chapter 3

pp. 40–41, "Is the organization . . .": Internal Revenue Service, U.S. Department of the Treasury, *Tax Guide for Churches and Religious Organizations*, "'Churches' Defined," http://www.irs.gov/charities/churches/article/0,,id=155746,00.html (accessed September 2, 2008).

p. 41, "As to the first criterion . . .": Bruce J. Casino, "Defining Religion in American Law," http://www.religiousfreedom.com/articles/casino.htm (accessed September 2, 2008).

pp. 42–43, "public welfare legislation . . .": *Everson* v. *Board of Education of Ewing Tp.*, 330 U.S. 1 (1947).

p. 43, "secular purpose . . .": *Lemon* v. *Kurtzman*, 403 U.S. 602 (1971).

p. 44, "deeply imbedded in the . . .": *Walz* v. *Tax Commission of the City of New York*, 397 U.S. 664 (1970).

p. 46, "part of the fabric . . .": *Marsh* v. *Chambers*, 463 U.S. 783 (1983).

p. 46, "far too late . . .": *Lynch* v. *Donnelly*, 465 U.S. 668 (1984).

Chapter 4

p. 52, "Both old and novel practices . . .": Feldman, 222.

p. 53, "The Regents recommended . . .": Feldman, 233.

p. 55, "In light of the history . . .": *School District of Abington Tp.* v. *Schemp*, 374 U.S. 203 (1963).

p. 55, "The Court held that . . .": *Wallace* v. *Jaffree*, 472 U.S. 38 (1985).

p. 59, "Journalists called it . . ." and "Newspapers also . . .": Clyde Wilcox and Carin Larson, *Onward Christian Soldiers? The Religious Right in American Politics* (Boulder, CO: Westview Press, 2006), 37–38.

p. 63, "There are two . . .": Phillip Johnson, interview by Joe McMaster, *Judgment Day: Intelligent Design on Trial*, PBS, April 6, 2007, http://www.pbs.org/wgbh/nova/id/defense-id.html (accessed September 2, 2008).

p. 63, "what science isn't very good . . .": Kenneth Miller, interview by Joe McMaster, *Judgment Day: Intelligent Design on Trial*, PBS, April 19, 2007, http://www.pbs.org/wgbh/nova/id/defense-ev.html (accessed September 2, 2008).

p. 64, "is a religious view . . .": *Tammy Kitzmiller, et al.* v. *Dover School District, et al.*, 04-cv-02688-JEJ, Doc. 342 (D.C. Penn. 2005).

p. 64, "a victory for . . .": Peter Slevin, "Kansas Education Board First to Back 'Intelligent Design,'" *Washington Post*, November 9, 2005, http://www.washingtonpost.com/wp-dyn/content/article/2005/11/08/AR2005110801211_pf.html

Chapter 5

p. 70, "In the light . . .": *McGowan* v. *Maryland*, 366 U.S. 420 (1961).

p. 72, "No state shall . . .": U.S. Constitution, amend. 14, sec. 1.

p. 75, "We are not pro-choice . . ": Jeff Fecke, "Seminarian Seeks to Bring Religious Support to Pro-Choice Movement," *Minnesota Monitor*, March 4, 2008, http://www.minnesotamonitor.com/showDiary.do?diaryId=3332 (accessed September 2, 2008).

pp. 77–78, "In a 2002 survey conducted by the Pew Forum . . .": The Pew Research Center for the People & the Press, "Public Makes Distinctions on Genetic Research," April 9, 2002, http://people-press.org/reports/display.php3?ReportID=152 (accessed September 2, 2008).

Chapter 6

p. 81, "A good deal of trouble . . .": Dean Acheson quoted in Madeleine Albright, *The Might & The Almighty: Reflections on America, God, and World Affairs* (New York: HarperCollins Publishers, 2006), 49.

p. 81, "The interests of a national . . .": George Kennan quoted in Albright, 49.

p. 85, "but I don't think we understood . . .": Stephen Prothero, "Religious Literacy: What Every American Should Know," Pew Forum Faith Angle Conference, Key West, FL, December 3, 2007, moderated by Michael Cromartie, http://pewforum.org/events/?EventID=162 (accessed September 3, 2008).

p. 86, "charity and compassion": cited in Stephen Kinzer, *Overthrow: America's Century of Regime Change from Hawaii to Iraq* (New York: Henry Holt, 2006), 157.

p. 86, "Let them burn . . .": quoted in Kinzer, 2006.

p. 89, "We were caught off guard . . .": Albright, 40.

p. 89, "When I was secretary of state . . ." and "Given the nature . . .": Albright, 75.

p. 90, "Whether religion is . . .": Douglas M. Johnston, "Faith Based Diplomacy: Bridging the Religious Divide," remarks to the Secretary's Open Forum, Washington, DC, December 8, 2006, U.S. Department of State, http://www.state.gov/s/p/of/proc/79221.htm (accessed September 3, 2008).

Chapter 7

p. 93, World religion piechart, Adherents.com, 2005, http://www.adherents.com/Religions_By_Adherents.html (accessed September 3, 2008). Reprinted with permission.

p. 96, "danger to the . . .": International Coalition for Religious Freedom, "Europe: Germany," *Religious Freedom World Report*, April 4, 2004, http://www.religiousfreedom.com/wrpt/Europe/germany.htm (accessed September 3, 2008).

p. 98, data for table: International Coalition for Religious Freedom, *Religious Freedom World Report*, 2004, http://www.religiousfreedom.com/ (accessed September 3, 2008).

p. 100, "Countries of Particular Concern": U.S. Department of State, "2006 Executive Summary," *International Religious Freedom Report 2006,* http://www.state.gov/g/drl/rls/irf/2006/71284.htm (accessed September 3, 2008).

p. 101, "self-determination" and "freely determine . . .": Office of the United Nations High Commissioner for Human Rights, *International Covenant on Civil and Political Rights,* 2200A (XXI), art. 1, cl. 1 (March 23, 1976) http://www2.ohchr.org/english/law/ccpr.htm (accessed September 3, 2008).

p. 102, "What's dangerous about . . .": Lisa Miller, "Moderates Storm the Religious Battlefield," *Newsweek,* Dec. 31, 2007/Jan. 7, 2008, 89.

Chapter 8

pp. 103–104, "All laws and regulations . . .": Jurist Legal Intelligence, "Constitution, Government, and Legislation," *Iran,* http://jurist.law.pitt.edu/world/iran.htm#Top (accessed September 3, 2008).

p. 105, "The lofty spirit . . .": quoted in Sandra Mackey, *The Iranians: Persia, Islam and the Soul of a Nation* (New York: Dutton, 1996), 334–335.

p. 109, "This is not a religious . . .": Frances Harrison, "'Mass Purges' at Iran Universities," *BBC News,* December 20, 2006, http://news.bbc.co.uk/2/hi/middle_east/6196069.stm (accessed September 3, 2008).

p. 112, "there has been . . .": Wilcox and Larson, 188.

Further Information

Further Reading

Bennett, Helen. *Humanism, What's That?* Amherst, NY: Prometheus Books, 2005.

Gold, Susan Dudley. *Engel v. Vitale: Prayer in the Schools.* Tarrytown, NY: Marshall Cavendish, 2006.

Karson, Jill. *Civil Liberties*, Chicago: Greenhaven Press, 2006.

Najar, Monica. *Evangelizing the South: A Social History of Church and State in Early America*, New York: Oxford University Press, 2008.

Patrick, John J. *The Supreme Court of the United States*, New York: Oxford University Press, 2006.

Websites

A Debate: Evolution v. Intelligent Design
http://www.pbs.org/wgbh/nova/id/program.html

Americans United for Separation of Church and State
http://www.au.org/site/PageServer

First Freedom First
http://www.firstfreedomfirst.org:80/

Religious Tolerance
http://www.religioustolerance.org/scs_intr.htm

Research Penn State: Separation of Church and State
http://www.rps.psu.edu/probing/religion.html

U.S. Department of State: Freedom of Religion
http://usinfo.state.gov/dd/eng_democracy_dialogues/religion/religion_essay.html

Bibliography

Albright, Madeleine. *The Mighty & The Almighty: Reflections on America, God, and World Affairs.* New York: HarperCollins Publishers, 2006.

Bowker, John. *Cambridge Illustrated History: Religions.* New York: Cambridge University Press, 2002.

Carter, Stephen L. *God's Name in Vain: The Wrongs and Rights of Religion in Politics.* New York: Basic Books, 2000.

——. *The Culture of Disbelief: How American Law and Politics Trivialize Religious Devotion.* New York: Random House, 1993.

Dreisbach, Daniel L. *Thomas Jefferson and the Wall of Separation Between Church and State.* New York: New York University Press, 2002.

Feldman, Stephen M. *Please Don't Wish Me a Merry Christmas: A Critical History of the Separation of Church and State.* New York: New York University Press, 1997.

Hamburger, Philip. *Separation of Church and State.* Cambridge, MA: Harvard University Press, 2002.

Mackey, Sandra. *The Iranians: Persia, Islam and the Soul of a Nation.* New York: Dutton Press, 1996.

Rawls, John. *Political Liberalism.* New York: Columbia University Press, 2005.

Wilcox, Clyde, and Carin Larson. *Onward Christian Soldiers? The Religious Right in American Politics.* Cambridge, MA: Westview Press, 2006

Index

Page numbers in **boldface** are illustrations, tables, and charts.

About the Author

KAREN JUDSON lives with her husband in the Black Hills of South Dakota. She is a former college biology instructor and has also taught high school science, kindergarten, and grades one and three. She has written about twenty books for young-adult readers, including *Animal Testing* and *Chemical and Biological Warfare*, both in Marshall Cavendish Benchmark's Open for Debate series. In her spare time she jogs, paints wildlife scenes, and designs quilts.